CW01240372

This signed, limited edition of

THE HUNGRY GODS

is one of 3,000 copies

SOLARIS

PRAISE FOR ADRIAN TCHAIKOVSKY'S NOVELLAS

"After reading *Ironclads*, I think I can count Tchaikovsky as one of my favourite authors. Highly recommended."

The Curious SFF Reader on *Ironclads*

"Tchaikovsky shows us yet again how versatile are his writing and storytelling."

Civilian Reader on *Walking to Aldebaran*

"Tchaikovsky focuses the taut story in such a way that every detail is relevant, building towards a climax that feels like a perfect pay-off."

SFX Magazine on *Firewalkers*

"This time-looped dramedy is as funny as it is thought-provoking."

Publishers Weekly on *One Day All This Will Be Yours*

"Tchaikovsky knocks it out the park… A cunning take on both fantasy tropes and heroes' journeys. He sticks the landing, too, with a last paragraph that perfectly pays off what came before it."

Locus Magazine on *Ogres*

"Once again shows Tchaikovsky's gift for worldbuilding… An amazing story on so many levels."

The British Fantasy Society on *And Put Away Childish Things*

"Has all the hallmarks of what makes the author's work so popular and award-winning: engaging, very well-written, and offers new twists on popular tropes. Highly recommended."

Civilian Reader* on *Ironclads

"By turns humorous and horrific. The scope of imagination on display is wonderful and I really didn't want to put this down."

The Fantasy Hive* on *Walking to Aldebaran

"A masterclass in concise storytelling… The book whips along at a rapid pace and characters are cleverly rendered. A fantastically easy read."

SciFiNow* on *Firewalkers

"An absurdly funny, sharply written novella… a must-read for genre newbies and sci-fi fans alike."

Starburst Magazine* on *One Day All This Will Be Yours

"Readers with a bent for social commentary and solving puzzles will be doubly pleased."

Publishers Weekly* on *Ogres

"I was quickly immersed in this delightful tale, finding boldness of concept, vividness of presentation and specialness of characters."

Locus Magazine* on *And Put Away Childish Things

THE HUNGRY GODS

Also by Adrian Tchaikovsky
from Solaris Books

Terrible Worlds: Revolutions
Ironclads
Firewalkers
Ogres

Terrible Worlds: Destinations
Walking to Aldebaran
One Day All This Will Be Yours
And Put Away Childish Things

After the War
Redemption's Blade

THE HUNGRY GODS

ADRIAN TCHAIKOVSKY

SOLARIS

First published 2025 by Solaris
an imprint of Rebellion Publishing Ltd,
Riverside House, Osney Mead,
Oxford, OX2 0ES, UK

www.solarisbooks.com

ISBN: 978-1-83786-551-2

Copyright © 2025 Adrian Czajkowski

The right of the author to be identified as the author of this work has been asserted in accordance with the Copyright, Designs and Patents Act 1988.

All rights reserved. No part of this publication may be reproduced, stored in a retrieval system, or transmitted, in any form or by any means, electronic, mechanical, photocopying, recording or otherwise, without the prior permission of the copyright owners.

This book is a work of fiction. Names, characters, places and incidents are products of the author's imagination or are used fictitiously.

10 9 8 7 6 5 4 3 2 1

A CIP catalogue record for this book is available from the British Library.

Designed & typeset by Rebellion Publishing
Cover art & illustration by Gemma Sheldrake

Printed in the UK

DRAMATIS PERSONAE

THE GODS

Guy Vesten—the Fallen God
Bruce Mayall—the Plant God
Matthias Fabrey—the Insect God
Padreig Gramm—the Plastics God

THE MORTALS

Amri—Rabbit people
Beaker—Seagull people
Iffy—Cockroach people
Remus—Rabbit people
Hailfoot—Rabbit people
Old Emma—Rabbit people
Chicori—Rabbit people
Failboy—Cockroach people

1.

RABBIT SCROUNGING

Amri hadn't wanted to scavenge the edge of the old city, but the well was dry again and the old streambeds of the high pastures were just trickles of muddy sludge. That meant everyone was on the hunt for water from worse places, no matter they'd have to boil it twice over before it was even safe to pour into the irrigation channels. No matter that any crops growing under that poison rain would taste like metal and turn your insides to runny butter. Better sick than starve, even though both killed.

A hard year for the Rabbit people, when even their patron starved. They'd scratched their living on the slopes above the city since anyone could remember, and the years had swung between hard and harder, but right now the sun was a cruel nail in the sky and the earth cracked and blew away on the hot wind. At the bottom of the well, when they'd let Amri down in the bucket, had been dust and small bones.

Yet there was always somewhere to scavenge, for water. The Clawfoot Pigeon people, who lived closer to the city on one side, had a great metal tank buried in the earth at the heart of their village that held a dozen years of rain, and sometimes they would trade. Remus had gone to them, because his second wife was one of their daughters. In a hard year everyone held onto what they had, but blood bought water—a truth that had become a saying, over the years.

And there was the sea, and days ago Hailfoot had gone with a handcart of cans and bottles, heading down the river to the great salt expanse of it. Salt, but it could be boiled, enough of it saved to keep a few meagre gardens green. And every poison river fed into the sea, but the sea was vast and the poison spread through it until you hardly got sick at all. Drink the river before it entered the city, and you'd be raving, vomiting, on your back with the shivers and seeing dead people. Drink it after it had coursed through that ravaged tangle of broken concrete and metal, plastic and tarmac, and you'd die. It took something as mighty as the sea to conquer the toxins and the heavy metals and the oily rainbow slick of it, and even then the sea struggled. The sea was full of tiny pieces of the old days, said Old Emma, just like all water was. They built up inside you, the more of the sea you drank. You got as old as Old Emma, then parts of you just plain stopped working, you coughed all the time and pissed blood. Everyone knew she'd not see her thirty-fourth winter.

Amri would rather have gone with Remus to the Clawfoot Pigeon and their watertank. She'd rather have gone with

Hailfoot and his weird, twitchy boy downriver to the sea, and risk the King Crab people and their hooked clubs and raiding boats. Rather any of that than the city.

Now here she was in the shadow of its outermost buildings, which had already been picked clean by scavengers who knew the ground better. The city was haunted, and *ate* Rabbits, everyone knew. Some said the ghosts ate them. Some said that it was the dogs, that had their own hierarchies and tribes, and parcelled out the innards of the city between them. Some said it was the rats, that were as big as dogs sometimes, and boiled up from the flooded world below, bristling with the diseases and poisons they had grown resistant to. Amri had a bow and a metal bladed knife, and she'd brave animals, because animals weren't brave. Amri was more worried about Seagulls. This was their place now, and they hated Rabbits coming to steal even the least that was theirs.

She'd argued, back at the village. She'd all but refused, but then she wouldn't have had her share even of the meagre stores they had left. But Amri was a Nothing from a Nobody family. One step above an outlaw. She and a handful of others from the list of the most despised were sent out each alone to gather not water, but fuel. Fuel to go under the constantly roiling cauldrons that turned bad water into less-bad water fit to go on crops, or the steam caught and condensed on the big tarpaulins to make water fit for drinking. Nobody went into the city for its vast sunken reservoirs of poison water, but there was still plenty to burn.

In Amri's mother's day, the Rat people had held this part of the city, and they had been fat and traded metal and wood, and kept gardens atop some of the stumps of ancient buildings. They'd had dances and celebrations, Amri had heard. On festival days you could look down from the hills and see a profligacy of fires strung from ruin to ruin. But they'd been soft, and the Seagull had come upriver in their boats and driven the Rat people deep into the city, where nobody went, or at least came back from. The Seagull, who traded for nothing but only took, except they hadn't been strong enough to stop the King Crab taking from *them*, and so had left their coastal haunts for easier pickings inland. Amri was profoundly scared of the Seagull. They offered human bodies to their patron, it was said. When the storms came in from the estuary and drove the white birds in wheeling, shrieking flocks over the vast expanse of ruin, the Seagull staked out their still-living prisoners with opened guts and invited their feathered cousins down to feast. Or so people said, and so Amri firmly believed.

But the city always had something to burn, and even though the ancient roads were cracked and broken, you could still wheel a cart down most of them.

"Even you," Old Emma had told her bitterly, "can come back with a heaped load of wood from the city. That is a task that is within the capabilities of even a Nothing like you. Or if the Seagull take you, that's one less mouth in a hard year."

I will just run, Amri had told herself when she set off down the mosaic road towards the city's edge. She'd said the same when she first camped, setting herself into the least space of an old house where the roof had fallen in, and mice fought vicious territorial wars over and beneath the decayed floors. And she'd snared three mice and imagined them pleading with her not to kill them in their inaudibly shrill voices, citing mouse children and elders they were responsible for, mouse dreams they'd had about their futures. And she, cruel and hungry god as she was to them, had killed them, skinned and gutted them, cooked their tiny carcases over her tiny fire and nibbled their bones. In her dreams that night she'd seen little mouse handcarts left, knocked askew and abandoned, heard the wailing of mouse families, and known no pity. If the Seagull caught her, if she fell into the city's carious below-spaces and broke a leg, nobody would wail for her. She was the least toe of the Rabbit.

I will just run, she told herself, as she entered the city proper—not just the vast scavenged ruinscape that extended up the hills in decreasing gradations of density, but that part where the tall bones of the ancient world still rose, the great rusted girders, the crazed concrete sagging in fractured indolence against corded iron cables. Where the ground crunched with tiny sharp pebbles that gleamed in the sun, not that the sun could fight its way down here very often. She had wrapped her rabbit-skin shoes with old cloth three times over, and she knew that she'd need to do it again each morning, because the constant abrasion of the sharp ground would chew into them with every step she took. Glass, it was called. Like the dirt of the hills, like the sand of the sea-beaches. Even the earth of the city had a razor-thirst for blood.

I will just run and never come back, she said on her way into the teeth of the city, but knew she wouldn't. What was a lone Rabbit, after all?

There was precious little on the hillsides that would burn which hadn't already been burned. What there was, they needed. Stunted little hedges whose roots held the fields together. The barriers that discouraged wild dogs and wilder vagrants. Even they were mostly plastic and metal, the bones of the old days. Every hard year was like a plague of locusts as the children of the Rabbit scoured for everything burnable within a rabbit's run of the village. Amri had done the same, when she was a child and it was the village's business to give her an easy run. Now she was grown, no close kin, no friends. To earn her place, she had to put her head in the snare.

End of the first day of scavenging and the little cart was mostly full. There was some loose wood left over from the old days here. The Seagull, and the Rat before them, weren't poor like the Rabbit. They didn't need to send their thin children out for every last seed and scrap. They collected water in tanks high on the stumps where they roosted that hardly needed boiling at all. Amri could creep into the lower floors of buildings and find where the rain hadn't turned everything to rot, and the groundwater hadn't crept its poison damp up the walls. Find desiccated boards of ancient furniture or wall panels, the crackling tinder of books that hadn't degraded yet, sifting rags of ancient cloth. All of it went on the cart. It would keep the fires going beneath the cauldrons. It would buy her shelter and food amongst her own people. Because in a hard year, the Rabbit gnawed at itself to escape starvation's trap. She was its least toe, first to go between its teeth. And she kept telling herself she'd leave, but the thought filled her with misery and terror.

Filling that much of a cart had emptied her whole day. Night was bringing on the dogs and the rats from their subterranean haunts. She wondered if the rodents remembered the people who'd borne their name and left them treats on festival days. She'd heard that the city's heart was home to Dog people, who lived and slept and hunted alongside the beasts, and warred constantly against one another. She wasn't sure she believed it, or who would be master in such an arrangement.

In the dusk she found herself a den on the third storey of a crumbling tower, one wall looking out into the dead sockets of its counterpart across the street, her cart hauled in tortuous stages up the crooked concrete steps. No fire, because that would be inviting the Seagull to come share it. She swept the ground as clear as she could of glass, laid her cloak down and put her pack beneath her head. And, past midnight with the pale moon leering in from a clear sky, she awoke and found three Seagulls standing about her.

Two were skinny youths and, if it had just been them, she might have fancied her chances. One thing the Rabbit knew was the value of a powerful kick to the nads and then headlong flight. But the third she knew, by reputation at least. He was an older man, lean, hair shaved down to white-streaked fuzz. Heavy-set, scarred, wearing a sleeveless jacket sewn with overlapping scales of hard plastic in a mosaic of white and red. What brought his name to her lips was the little affectation balanced on his nose, twin discs of glass with metal rims that made his face cruel and distant, something other than human. They called him Beaker. He was the only Seagull whose name she knew. He was champion, priest and executioner, eater of the dead, torturer of the living, the monster that Amri's generation scared children with.

"My boys," he said in a soft voice, "we seem to have caught ourselves a fish." The Seagull still had a rolling accent from when they'd lived downriver by the sea, not speaking as the Rabbit and Cockroach and Clawfoot Pigeon did, or as the Rat had. Back home, people made fun of the way the Seagull stretched the sounds of their speech, but it didn't seem funny now. His magnified eyes ranged over her, seeing a skinny girl in tattered sheeting and furs, feet wrapped in abraded cloth she hadn't taken off from the day before, a yellow scarf about her neck. Her loaded cart was between her and them, but it wasn't as though she'd be getting out with it now.

But maybe she could still get out. Up on the third floor, yes, but better that than the Seagull staking her out for their patron to gorge on. She did the Rabbit trick that always surprised everyone, going from a still start to full-pelt dash without transition. One of the kids lunged for where she'd started off and got her foot in the side of his head—more than she'd hoped for and it gave her something more to push away from, an extra iota of speed. The other one had paused, so his grab for her was better aimed, but even then she was moving faster than he'd thought. She felt his fingers claw at her calves and slapped back, the blade of her hand clipping the top of his head. For a moment she seemed to hang between those two transient contacts, then he was behind her. She was in the gaping void of a window, feeling sharp stubs of glass under her palms as she vaulted out. Out into the empty air. Out into a drop, but *out*. The Rabbit ran first, planned later, because the world was built on the bones of people who stopped to think too much.

And then he had her ankle. Beaker's hand like a knot of vines, like it had grown there over a hundred years, set down roots, never to be removed. And then the yank, even as she was four-fifths out over the abyss. A whipcrack reversal of momentum and the jagged rim of the window tore up her smock and grazed her belly. Her jaw clacked on the edge and she bit her tongue and cheek. By the time she was sitting at Beaker's feet she was too dazed and hurting to know how much trouble she was in.

"Bitch," hissed the boy she'd kicked. He kicked her back and she folded around her gut, though her jaw was shouting loud enough to eclipse any amateur theatrics like that. She felt tears in her eyes and blood sticky on her chin. And then Beaker's fingers, dabbling in it, tilting her head so she saw her twin reflections in his lenses. She looked already dead, in those little simulacra. A gory severed head twice over.

"Little Run-Rabbit," Beaker said.

"Please," she got out, muffled by the pain in her jaw. "I'll pay. Pay for wood." Except the Seagull didn't trade. But what else did she have?

"Way I see it, flower, is that we have you already. Nothing here that doesn't belong to us already." His voice was quiet, reasonable. Were there Seagull children who listened to that voice tell them stories of an evening? A woman in whose ear he whispered endearments? She clutched desperately at the thought, seeking some commonality she could use as a tool to pry herself from this trap. There was no way into the details of his life for her, though.

"Bring her on, lads," he said, and his lackeys lifted her between them. Not down to a Rabbit's ground but higher, to the broken-tooth crown of the ruined tower, its labyrinthine inner structure laid bare in ankle-high ridges where internal walls had been.

"You sought the sky," Beaker told her. They dumped her down right at the building's lip—five storeys up now, beyond any hope of surviving the fall. "That seems an omen, to me. Run-Rabbit's place is in the earth. Do you still want the sky, Run-Rabbit?"

"Please." Amri was shivering, not just from the night chill. Above them all the sky was cloudless, like unfiltered black water still swimming with gleaming particles of grit.

"Ask the gods something from me." Beaker was crouched right beside her, his lips, her ear. "Have them send me a sign to help me understand it all."

"I'll have them send you a pox," Amri spat, the absolute limit of her defiance. And he was right there, balanced on the balls of his feet. She could have grabbed him and hauled him over the edge with her, if she was going anyway. But that would take more than a Rabbit's courage.

He chuckled. "Tell them Beaker sent you. They will honour you for that."

And then the sky lit on fire.

Trails of it, streaking low overhead, turning the black to red. And then the thunder, as though lightning had started and forgotten to stop. A roaring that shook the building beneath them, shook the city around them, and the world beyond that. And Amri had seen shooting stars before, that the elders said were some last pieces of the old world finally meeting its fiery end, but not like this. Not bellowing out its rage as it fell to the earth, but *slowly*. Four fierce fists of fire roaring fury at all the world as they descended from heaven. Falling into the city. Falling into the heart of ruin. Even falling towards the hillsides of the Rabbit people.

She glanced at Beaker. He was staring and the sky-fire gleamed in the cracked lenses over his eyes.

The world was ending, but in that moment *her* world still lived and her feet still worked and she was up and past Beaker, past his lackeys and back down the concrete stairs. Round and round like some obscure religious devotion, every two turns taking her down a floor, ten turns bringing her to the street. No cart, nothing to show for all her time save a whole skin. A mostly whole skin. And she'd take it. She'd live with it, and with the scorn of the others, if it meant that she would live.

The first shout came from above, the Seagull collecting themselves. By then she was already running down the street, feeling her worn foot-bindings shred against the ground-glass city soil. Let a Rabbit run, though, and you'd lost them. No faster pair of heels in all the world. By the time Beaker and his friends had reached the ground, she was long gone and still going.

2.

THE GREENING

THE NEXT MORNING the sky was painted with smoke. She'd run most of the night—it felt like that, anyway—then holed up in a half-buried cellar that felt like one more shock would seal it up entirely. Better death in the earth than the Seagull finding her again. But the night had already used up its supply of shocks—and the whole next year's too, by Amri's estimation.

If Beaker was casting about for her trail, he never picked it up again. The Rabbit had come through for its least little toe after all. *If in doubt, always run.*

She woke with the idea that she could at least scavenge an armful of wood, have something to show for the trip. When she went outside, the smoke was so big it filled her eyes, shoving all other thoughts out of her head, and shunting them aside into the forever. Plumes of it, two within the city and two off towards the hills. Not like a bonfire rising up, but the tracks of things that had come down.

There were things in the sky, everyone knew. The ancient people had put them there. You saw them most nights, swift-moving stars crossing from horizon to horizon as you watched, set against the other points of light that took a year to make their slow revolution. There had been more swift stars once. Every generation a few fell. Was this what it was like when they fell *on* you? But four together wasn't something anyone had ever seen.

It began to rain. Rain, that hadn't come forever, so that the Rabbit fields had dried, and everyone down to the children had been set fetching water, or fuel to boil it with. A harsh, acrid rain, as though the thundering apparitions of the night had shaken it loose from the highest reaches of the sky. Torn the jealous rain deities a new one and stolen their bounty, to scatter it across the earth in profligate abandon.

Beaker had spoken about omens. That was a thing for the Seagull. Rabbits never sought deep truths in the world. You looked for what you needed, and if there was a greater truth to the world then you hoped it passed you by. The meaning of life was surviving until tomorrow. The world was built on the bones of people who'd wanted more than that.

But this... How could this be anything *other* than meaning? It was almost enough to have her go seek out Beaker again. A man who knew his omens, even if he was made of murder and pain. She felt a desperate need to understand what had happened to her world.

Whatever had happened, some of it had happened off towards the village, and her feet were already dragging her back there. She had to see. She had to know. Empty-handed, she walked the broken roads out of the city, back up the dry hillsides towards Rabbit country.

SHE ALMOST MADE it. She was almost in time to be too late.

The Rabbit had built their village high on a slope. Fields spread in ragged tiers below, bounded by retaining walls of old-world detritus fitted carefully together, bowed by the shift of earth but still holding. The fields had been dry and wilting when she had left; they were overflowing now because it hadn't stopped raining all the long way back from the city. What had seemed a novelty at first had become one more thing to be endured. The rain tasted oily and metallic and stung her eyes. As though the falling stars had left poisoned air behind them, and the rain that dropped through it came out tainted and wrong. Yet right, somehow. As she approached the village she saw something was happening to the road and the shells of buildings around her. A flowering, a growing. Shoots pushing their way between the cracks of tarmac and concrete. Roots gripping at old stone and tumbled brick, breaking apart and binding together in equal measure. Flowers out of season, opening with unnatural rapidity. A hundred thousand tiny bursts of life unfolding, fast enough for her to see them move.

Up ahead she could see her people, though none of them had eyes for her. There were Rabbits out in the fields, rejoicing at half-dead crops that were suddenly springing into mad, tangled life. Wilted leaves unfurling like old men rediscovering the virility of their youth. Children with open arms, trying to catch the rain, opening their mouths and then spitting because what came from the sky was chemical and foul. *But only to us,* Amri understood. *To the plants it's nectar.*

She was waving. A dreadful urgency was in her. Only later did she understand that her feet were screaming dread to her. The threadbare bindings almost worn through, her soles listening to the shake in the earth.

Beyond the fields, within the village, the smoke. The trail of whatever had come down. She could see people there, gathered around a crater that had destroyed three houses, compounding ruin on ruin. It seemed weirdly contained to Amri. She had seen the fiery thing coming down with its kin, like the end of days. How had it made so small a dent in the world?

The ground was still shaking beneath her, and her heart caught suddenly, an abject terror she had no words for. The Rabbit had one rule. *If you want to see tomorrow, you run.* But nobody was running. They were gathering close around this new thing, the one thing you never did. *If it's strange, you run. You always run.* Leave it to Rats and Seagulls to be curious. But here was a strangeness so big it filled the whole world, so nobody was running. The fire, the falling thing, the smoke, the rain. Her people's grasp on the world had been stretched until it broke and now they were curious, joyous even, when they should be running.

Amri was running, by then, but she was running *towards*. Even she had forgotten the teachings of the Rabbit.

The first explosion enveloped the heart of the village and the crowd that had gathered there. She skidded to a halt, waiting for the thunder that must surely come, interpreting the vast overshadowing hand thrown up as just more smoke or dust, an insubstantial pall that the rain and air would carry away. Nothing substantial. It *couldn't* be, not just erupting out of the earth like that.

She could hear the screaming, thin and distant on the breeze. The stinging rain changed direction to dagger at her face. It wasn't smoke.

A vast excrescence of fungal fronds had ripped free of the earth where the star had fallen, and at its base a chaotic tangle of roots and vines, lashing out as though suddenly released from an impossibly compacted prison. Amri had no clear view of what happened to the closest of her kin there, but the vines were thick as human bodies and in constant, mashing motion. They ground and knotted against each other, strangling and twisting and crushing, expanding outwards to colonise the old ruins the village was built on, to pulverise the fragile walls of the houses, root into the cellars. Obliterate every trace of her people as though they had never been. Only cracked skulls and bloody ribs left, caught amongst the riot of new growth. In that instant, everything stopped. Amri, on the road. All the jubilant men and women and children in the fields. The sun in its orbit. Her heart in her chest. An instant of utter stillness in the echo of that sudden, impossible flowering.

Then the great clutch of vegetal life seemed to contract for a moment, as though bracing itself. In the next heartbeat it was rushing outwards in all directions at the speed of a running man, faster. Not moving like an animal, not even reaching out with the gnarled maze of roots it had already thrown up. Just more of it, tearing free of the ground all around. Bloated mushrooms lanced from the earth like spears and unfurled caps ten feet across, twenty feet in the air. Snarls of leaves edged with jagged teeth flung themselves from tight-balled fists to jagged efflorescences larger than a man, shearing through anything that got in their way. Thigh-thick brambles, studded with hooks like raptor talons, coursed over the fields like joyous hounds, looping into the air and then coming to earth where they split into a half-dozen more. Amri was screaming now, telling the Rabbit to run, the one thing nobody should need to be told. And they were running. Everyone who had been far enough outside the village's heart to escape that first bloody harvest. They ran, but the appallingly accelerated growth was faster. Not even chasing them, just venting from the ground beneath them, boiling out from some vegetable hell, driving shoots through flesh, twisting hard briars about bone, drinking up the blood and then lifting red leaves in worship to the rain-dimmed sky.

In less time than it took for her to understand what she was seeing, the whole village was gone, burst apart and torn down and overgrown and buried, as though time had run forward faster than any rabbit and she was seeing a world of a million tomorrows brought impossibly to today. The houses, the fields, the people, all obliterated and replaced by thriving, angry plant life. If she had run faster, or even just got up earlier that morning, she would have been in the heart of it. She'd have been in that crowd, telling them of her adventures.

She stopped running. There was nothing to run to. Everything of her people was gone, everything she'd known.

The growth was slowing. Still approaching, but each new flowering was pushing from the earth with less urgency, unfolding with a gathering laziness and to less effect. What burst out close to her toes was merely... grass, a handful of mushrooms the size of her thumbnail, a dotting of hardy weeds.

Amri stared. She had no more run left in her. She was left with two realities: *her* world and *the* world, and the one had been devoured by the other.

She dropped to her knees. *Always run*, but there weren't any Rabbits anymore so what did it matter what the rules were? She felt the scream building in her, the wailing, the denial, the tears. As though they belonged to someone else, to the part of her body that didn't think or feel. Just things that had to be done through adherence to tradition, because she was numb. She had no connection to any of it. Everything that bound her to the world was severed.

Then the voice, from behind her. Speaking words she didn't immediately understand. An accent stranger than the rolling vowels of the Seagull. Words said three times, slower and clearer with repetition, until she understood that they *were* words and came from another human being and weren't just a madness in her head.

"Don't stay there. It hasn't finished growing."

A stranger, pale, square-faced. Tall and strong-framed, wearing clothes of metal and plastic, but not pieced-together fragments. A reinforced suit to cover his body, all of a piece. In one hand, a hard dome with a clear faceplate that she identified as a helmet.

"I don't understand," she whispered.

He took her arm and she shivered. His fingers were like cold stones and there was a terrible strength there, not exerted against her flesh but she could feel the potential. He drew her back away from what had been her village, and wasn't, and would never be anymore.

"The gods have come back to Earth," he told her, with a nod at the murderous verdancy that had devoured her people.

"How do you know?" she whispered.

"Because I am one."

3.

THE FALLEN ONE

Everything in Amri was screaming to run away. A grand and terrible thing had eclipsed everything she ever knew. It was still there. Unlike regular nightmares, it hadn't even had the decency to return to the earth from whence it came. The whole unthinkable fungal abundance of it was before her, still swaying slightly from the violence of its creation. And now this man.

Tall, chiselled, alien. Not of her people, or the Seagull who'd come off the coast, or even the King Crab. She'd seen a King Crab once, a woman of a different palette, face pulled and pushed by different bones. This man was different all over again. And a god, self-professed.

She'd thought she knew what gods were. They were invisible things, spread thin across all of what they claimed. Gods were like the other half of a circle started by people. Prayer fed the gods, and the gods sent ideas and dreams to feed people. Rabbit told its people, *Run*, and Seagull, *Raid*.

And she wondered what would become of Rabbit now the prayers had stopped. The god must still be there, stretched between all the actual rabbits in the world, but without people to give divinity shape, that sounded like something less than a gossamer shimmer in the air.

"A god," she managed.

"*Ah gawd*," he echoed, trying out the way she said the words. "As much of one as you'll ever see, little one." He spread his arms out wide and turned about as he spoke, as though a multitude of worshippers surrounded them. "Let it be known that on this day the ancient creator deities returned to the world that gave birth to them, to take the dry dust of a dead land and breathe life back into it. To remake the world in all its glory from the dry bones that were all that was left." And by that point he'd revolved back to face her. "Which makes me ask who you are. And who were they?" A flip of the hand towards the louring vegetable horror that had consumed her village.

"We're the Rabbit," Amri got out. Her legs were suddenly weak and she sat down, feeling her shoulders shake. "We're the Rabbit. I'm the Rabbit's least toe. I'm Amri. Everyone knows I'm the worst of us. Why am I still here? Why am I here and they're all gone?" For a moment she teetered on the brink of believing that *she* was dead and, elsewhere in the true world, everyone else was going on with their lives. She was dead and this monstrosity was what you saw when you were dead, just like weird men who said they were gods. That made more sense than the other way round. She could have clung to that belief if he hadn't started laughing.

"The…?" He doubled over as much as the hard plates of his suit would permit. "*Rabbit?* Seriously? Rabbit? You cling on, on a dead planet, and the best you can do is rabbits? Were Roach and Rat taken?"

"Roach's people live that way," she spat. "Rat got driven away when the Seagull came."

He blinked. "There are more of you?"

"They're not *of me!* They're Seagulls. They kill us. They almost killed me!" And it was his utter ignorance of these integral world truths that convinced her she wasn't dead. Because she didn't know what waited to greet the dead when they passed on but, if there was anything at all, it would at least know the ways of the world. It would know the Rabbit, if only to mock them for their running. "Did you make this happen? How do you not know these things?"

She staggered to her feet and lunged at him, the thing you only did as a Rabbit if you had nowhere left to run. She beat her fists against his hard plastic suit, feeling solid muscle underneath. When he shoved her away, she ended up on her backside in the dust.

He raised his hands and she flinched, but he spread them to show he meant no harm.

"Guy," he said. "Guy Vesten." As though the name should mean as much to her as Rabbit should to him. "I came from space." As though the word should mean anything at all. And her blankness was on full display in her face, because he rolled his eyes and pointed at the sky. "Beyond what you see up there. Past the moon. Past some of the planets—the moving stars? From space. We went to space. And now we're back."

She blinked. "We…? You and… that?" At the centre of the invasive mass of growth, corrugated fans of fungal matter quivered and waved, and poisonous blooms opened petals of violent hues.

"And more," Guy said. "We are all that's left of a world you probably can't even imagine. But we're the pinnacle of it, too. That's why we survived. The greatest minds of Earth's glorious past. Earth, this world we're on. You're all living in our ruins." Frustrated because she couldn't instantly see things the way he did. "This was a city once. All of this."

"City," she echoed. This much she understood. "That's the city." Pointing back towards Seagull territory and the far brown smear of the river.

"This *all* was. You're just living the suburban dream out here." Meaningless words that seemed to amuse him. And then the whole vegetal conurbation shuddered, and a new explosion of racing roots tore up the earth another hundred paces, throwing up snarls of thorns and lurid, semitranslucent toadstools taller than a man. Amri shrieked and skittered further away, and she saw Guy back off as well. Not so much of a god as all that, then.

"Make it stop!" she shouted at him. "You did this, then stop it!" She had a vision of being chased all the way back to the Seagull with this devouring horror at her heels the whole way.

"Not me," Guy said. The humour had gone. "The others. One of the others. Fucking *Vegemate*." One more nonsense word. "Let's put some distance between us and this... excess."

THEY'D TRAVELLED WHAT seemed like miles and miles, but the great sails of the fungal kingdom were still visible when they paused, taller than the grandest stump of the old city. Amri had taken Guy towards Clawfoot Pigeon territory. Close enough that she could see their stockade of jagged metal, painted white and toxic with the droppings of their birds. Would they take a lone Rabbit in? Pigeon's doctrine was to build and feed families. Perhaps that was where her future lay. Except she had been sidetracked into becoming the disciple of Guy Vesten, the god-man.

He had food, though. Sticks of something that tasted like shock but made her feel full. He could take a stone and make it too hot to touch; she could warm herself by it like a fire. When she found a pool of oily murk, he could even decant that into his suit and have it spit out stale-tasting water. Right then, these were all the claims to godhood that Amri needed.

"There were four of us," he told her, as they sat within three walls of a tumbled house and she warmed herself by the stone. "The greatest minds of our time. Pioneers, innovators. The men who shaped the world, who gave people everything they wanted, things they didn't even realise they needed until we created them. Because it takes a special mind to see a thing that doesn't exist and understand how it completes people's lives. Earth's last golden age,

Amri." Reclining back against the stones, gesturing with one bare hand, his gauntlets in his lap. "When I have the tech running, I'll show you images. Of what we had, what we built. And what we left, I suppose."

"Why left?" She was watching him warily, keeping the stone between them like it was a fire and he was a threat. Because he was a threat, if he wanted to go for her. She could tell already how strong he must be. Broad shoulders, long arms, bigger and burlier than any human being she had ever seen. He'd be a whole head over Beaker even, big enough to break the Seagull's murder-champion in two.

He cocked his head back, staring up at the sky. The rain had long ceased, but there were clouds gathering again—in particular back over the fungus and the plants, a slow revolving dance of thunderhead grey. They needed rain and moisture, Guy had said. And, because they were the province of a god, even the weather could be made to oblige.

"We left," he said, "because the world was dying. Exhausted, mined out, poisoned. Despite our best efforts, despite everything we'd done to make people's lives better, the damage had already been done. We could see the future, gods as we were. And, because we were gods, we could *make* the future, too. A future in other places than the crippled world we had been born into. And so we left this world and went into space and built our paradise. A new world to our specifications, with none of the ingrained flaws that had destroyed the old. A world where people would be free to live without shackles and barriers." His smile lit the world around him, as though the golden glory of that utopia was reflected there. "We saved everything we could. Nobody could have done more."

"Four of you."

"We four, and those who shared our vision, who had courage enough to cut themselves loose from the old world. Our picked people, the experts, the geniuses, the hard workers. The worthy. But most of all, we four."

"Sounds great," Amri said sourly.

"It was." Her sarcasm hadn't registered. "We built something truly special between us. But at last the time came when we knew we had to come back. We had a duty, you see. Our lost home, this ruin of a world. Once we had finished making heaven in space, we knew we had to return. To restore life to this dead planet. To create a second heaven, here on Earth." A grand gesture to indicate the overgrown landscape of fallen buildings around them, with such assurance that Amri felt all her memories of her own people, her personal history, tremble and gutter.

"It's not dead," she said. "We live here." *Lived* here, her mind corrected.

"If you could have seen the world from space," he said, as though it was an answer and not just a non sequitur. "Back at the height of things, the continents spangled with the lights of cities, strung together by busy roads. The whole globe coursing with threads and clusters of light." The light that glimmered in his face as he spoke seemed to have been cast there from a lost and elder age. It faded as he added, "And how it looked when we came back. A dark world.

A dead world. Deserts, poisoned lakes, oceans bleached of fish. The ruin that we fled, progressed to its final stage. A blank canvas, we thought. But here you are, somehow. A handful of rabbits, clinging on with your little paws. And now not even that. I'm sorry."

She tried to assay whether the pause before that apology made the words fake. "You can't…" she tried, although maybe there wasn't actually anything he *couldn't*. "You can't just…" Jabbing a hand out into the darkness towards where her village had been. And it wasn't mere memory or guesswork. Whole swathes of that mycological jungle were glowing corpselight pale in the night, casting a cool swath of light across the earth and the underside of the clouds. It had grown, too. Where she had stood, to see the ruin of everything she knew, was already gone, and another hundred yards of ground beyond it. Morning would bring another burst of ravening growth, she guessed. "That," she said. "How is *that* anything of what you're saying. *That*'s making the world better?"

"Not my plan. Vegemate's plan." And, at her blank look, "That's what we called him. Bruce. Bruce Mayall. He was always the plant guy. Hydroponics and engineering for harsh conditions. Garden cities. Green spaces in space. But he took it too far. Obsessive. Like they all got." He turned a haunted expression on her. "When we made our plans to come back, we discovered that we weren't united in our dream anymore. We'd been off perfecting our particular technologies. Our special areas of interest. And when it came to bringing life back to the old planet, we found we'd... diverged. Bruce wanted to rewild the world. Make the Earth green again. This is the start of it, the seed. And he'll keep growing, exponentially. Tearing up every brick and girder of what was left and making it his garden. Unless the others stop him. Or I do. And they're just as bad. Worse. I need to go see what they're cooking up soon enough. But it won't be anything good for you, or your people."

"I don't *have* people," Amri said dully. "Anymore."

For a moment he didn't even understand what she meant, but that was because *she* hadn't understood what *he* meant. "Your people," he repeated. "All the people. Whatever scraps of people have clung on, on this planet. These Seagulls and Pigeons and Roaches and goddamn Capybaras or whatever the hell you've got here. All of them. Bruce is going to keep expanding until it's all fungus and trees as far as the eyes can see, every continent brought back to life, every latitude conquered. Life and decay chasing each other's tails forever. And him in the middle of it, plant god of the new green world. Jesus fucking Christ." Shaking his head. "Portrait of the Earth as a giant legume."

"And what were you going to do?"

His eyes were hooded when he turned back to her. "It doesn't matter, does it?" he asked, all that regret and wonder just banished and only bitterness left. "Because they cast me out."

She stared.

"You see before you the rogue of the pantheon, Amri," Guy said. "Because I tried to stop them doing things like *this*."

A gesture towards the pallid glow on the horizon. "Because I tried to remind them of what it meant to be human, rather than what they'd become. Because I *did* remind them of that, and they didn't appreciate it. They sabotaged my machines, destroyed my terraforming engines, cast me to Earth and assumed I'd burn all the way down until I broke against the ground." His face had become terribly hard, all jagged angles in the fading ember glow. "But I lived. All they left me with was this body, this mind. But I've built futures with this mind, and the body's top notch. I grew it to my own specs. I lived, and I will make them regret it. I'm going to fight them for the future of the Earth, and you and your people are going to help me."

And she wanted to tell him again that she had none, but he was using that other meaning of the word 'people,' including outsiders and enemies and tribes she hadn't even heard of, because what were insuperable gulfs of difference to her were just scratched lines in the dirt to him, and just as easily erased.

4.

SCRAPS OF FUR

THE MORNING BROUGHT bad news and good. Bad, because the spreading kingdom of the plant god definitely covered more ground, even though the rate of its expansion had slowed. Amri wondered if Rabbit's lesser children had found an accommodation with it, and were even now creeping under its shadow and gnawing at its stems. Perhaps the Rabbit had let its people die because the hopping, burrowing animals dear to its heart would thrive in this new god-altered world. Was it her duty to let it, in that case? Or to bow to the demands of this new vegetal deity? Who was she, Amri, to go against the will of a god, no matter how murderous and strangely named?

The good news was that people came to see what had happened because, of all divine attributes, subtlety was one that the god of plants did not possess. His arrival, growth and pallid radiance had brought a handful of the Clawfoot Pigeon out from behind their walls, and with them was their children torn up and crushed by a tragedy bigger than his imagination could hold.

He didn't howl, weep, beat at his breast. He didn't run, either. He sat, dead-faced, as Amri stumbled over what little explanation she could make, details of her clash with the Seagull tumbling into what she found on her return as though her tongue was reluctant to face up to this terrible newness that had come into the world.

"Gods?" Remus whispered. "Why would gods want to kill us? What did we ever do to attract the wrath of the gods?"

"It's not like that," Guy broke in on his grief. "My mate Bruce didn't even know you existed, not really. But he'd have been looking for a seed fund of biomass to get things started. I came down first. I was even on my way to your village when Vegemate picked his spot. You had fields planted. Probably that was why. Biomass." Interweaving words Amri knew with those she didn't, all said with such confidence that his meaning came over nonetheless.

"Did our crops... anger the plant god?" Remus asked helplessly.

"More like pleased him," Guy said philosophically. "Snacks to let him bootstrap to this level of growth. And still going. You're Remus, then? Who are these with the feathers?"

The handful of Pigeons had been watching them all distrustfully. They gave names, but Amri was too distracted to hold onto them.

"They're this fighting tribe you were having problems with?" Guy asked her.

She frowned, because there were things you'd expect a god to know. "The Seagull live in the city. These are the Pigeon. We trade, sometimes."

Then Remus was shouting, up on his feet, waving, and she saw a lone figure shuffling along the cracked road from the direction of the village. Of where the village had been. A woman close to Amri's age. Her name was Chicori, and she'd been out at the edge of the fields when everything happened, and had obeyed the Rabbit's last and greatest command and run, fast enough that the vines had scratched her heels but not caught her.

Another couple of stragglers turned up later, and then down from the coast road came Hailfoot and his boy, hauling a cart of dried fish and seawater from their trading down the coast, and that meant there were all of seven Rabbits left in the world. Twice as many of the Pigeon had come, too, carrying spears and slings. By that evening there was quite the gathering around the fire someone lit, staring out at the glowing excrescence of the plant god's kingdom and talking in low voices.

Guy hopped up on a mound of worn bricks. Something on his suit made a shrill, ear-drilling noise that smothered every other conversation and drew all eyes to him.

"The gods have returned," he told them all. "I know the girl here's told a little, as she understands it. Four men, god-men. Men of the time when this place was a real city and there were a million people living within sight of just this house we're in right now. We left because the world was dying. We returned to bring it back to life. Four gods, but three evil ones, and me.

"You've seen what's out there. What my man Vegemate Bruce has done to your people. And will keep doing, spreading further and further until he's turned the whole world into his garden. The other two are going to be just as bad in their own way, believe me. Three wicked gods, and me, who they cast out of their company because I told them no." And he stood there, bigger and stronger than anyone they ever saw, in his impossible armoured clothes. A ring of lights about the neck of his suit lit his face up so they could all see those angular features, exactly like some faded icon or image of the old times. Who could doubt what he said?

"Your days on the Earth are done," Guy told them flatly. "Or they are if my fellow gods have their way. There's no room for you in the new Earths they've dreamt up. But there's hope. Because you've got me. I am the god of people. With me, you can fight back against Vegemate and the others. Beat them. Because I know them, and I know where some of the cracks are. Believe me, at the end we were all trying to find out how to screw each other over. Once it was clear nobody's ideas about how to revive the Earth matched anyone else's. And they got to me first, sabotaged me in orbit, thought I'd burn up and die on re-entry. But they failed, and that means I'm here telling you you've got a chance. If you fight. If you do what I say."

Amri felt his words resound in her, despite herself. Despite the world of yesterday telling her: *Rabbits run; they don't fight.* There was an almost obscene confidence in Guy's voice. A god's confidence. The world had a thousand ways to put stones under your feet, ground glass in your food and poison in your water. Even without malevolent gods descending to obliterate whole villages, the world wanted to cut and sicken and kill you. But that was her world, not Guy's. When he spoke about how things would be, she could almost feel the world knuckling under and moving aside so he could get his way.

Perhaps she was more taken with him than the others, though. That morning, the Pigeon left. They shook their heads, and they offered to let Remus—just Remus—come with them, because he had married into their people and they liked him.

"We will trust our walls," they said. "Trust our walls and not visit here again."

"It's still growing," Guy told them. "And it'll tear up your walls when it gets there. It'll be sudden. One day you'll see the green and the fungus outside, then overnight everything you've built will be gone. Ask the girl here how fast that stuff can grow."

"As fast as a rabbit running!" Amri agreed.

But the Clawfoot Pigeon turned their backs and left.

"I don't reckon they'd have been much use, anyway," Guy said, watching them depart. "We need fighters, not whatever sad birds they were. We need an army, to keep my mate Bruce on his toes and take up his attention."

He reached out and had Amri's shoulder before she could flinch away. "Now, you tell me about this mob you were having all the problems with. We can go get *them* to fight for us. They sound punchy."

She shrank back, but she couldn't squirm from his grip. "The Seagull will never," she said. "They hate us." Because that was easier than saying that they just looked down and spat on the Rabbit as cowards and prey.

"We can use that," Guy said philosophically. "You and me, we're going to teach them a lesson about what you do when you meet a god." His grin again, like the sun. "And then they'll come round to our side of things and go fight for our side. Get your things; you can show me the way."

5.

TREES SPEAKING

Dawn would see them heading west towards the city again, retracing her panicked flight. A flight that had brought her home just in time to see the end of everything she knew. But the night had more to offer.

Amri wasn't able to sleep. The other survivors of the Rabbit seemed to have just collapsed the moment the sun was down and the fire lit. Amri should have been dead on her feet herself. Her shivering night spent on the fringes of the city seemed a hundred years away now. But when she closed her eyes, she saw the shocking violence of the plants, the earth broken asunder by roots and briars. She saw the vast fungal sails unpack themselves to blot out the sun. She saw skulls and red shreds of meat dance amongst the thickening coil of vines before being swallowed out of sight. Every part of her wanted to sleep except her memory, which dreaded the very thought and needled her awake, eyes wide open as though they'd never shut again.

And so she saw it when Guy, who had been sitting cross-legged overlooking the camp, stood up and walked off. A spike of fear yanked at her. Was he abandoning them? Was he betraying them? He was headed back the way they'd come, to where her life had once been and the killing fields of the new god were now. They had been friends together once, he'd said. Peers of the same four-man pantheon. And the fallings-out of gods were beyond her imagination, but perhaps he had decided that humility was the better part of valour. Was he returning to the fold?

She trailed him up the rising country to where the great crown of new life clutched. It had grown, obliterated the furthest outlying fields and boundary markers her people had put down. Other than herself and the handful of other survivors, there were no signs that the Rabbit had ever existed. She even saw their namesake dead there, little sad bags of fur and bones caught in strangling snares of whiplash creeper. Snapped up in toothed leaves, drowned in liquid-filled pits with greased cellulose walls. The plant kingdom was defending itself against all that would eat it.

And the great conurbation of foliage was not spreading equally, she saw. It had begun to put out a great pseudopod of rampant expansion, reaching hungrily downslope. Towards the old dead city, its poisoned water and its Seagull people. As though the plants were aggressively seeking to cleanse the Earth of all traces of past humanity, as if consuming all of the Rabbit hadn't even taken the edge off their hunger.

Guy walked past the fringes, just a few steps further than Amri dared follow him. He veered aside from nothing, stretched a long step over some other nothing, the unseen hair triggers that would doubtless unleash some vegetable trap to make an end of intruders.

He rolled his shoulders, and his shoulders flew off.

In the wan moonlight that was what she saw. The plastic shoulders of his clothes spread filmy, flickering wings and launched themselves up into the air. She saw he had smaller, more regular shoulders beneath them. The fliers were servants, machines that did his will, just as the old people of the long-ago days had possessed. The people whose inheritor he claimed to be.

He stood there, arms outstretched. She saw light glimmer and dance before his face, pictures drawn in the air there. His little flying servants were lost in the dark now, but she guessed they were speaking to him somehow, showing him what they could see.

Amri's first thought was that it was all a frightening kind of magic. That was what the Rabbit would tell her. It was strange, so it was a threat and she wanted none of it. Except when the real threat had come, what had Rabbit done for its people? They hadn't even had the chance to run away.

The flying things came back at last. Guy held his hands up, cupped, and they deposited things there, let down by little articulated limbs and claws. Fruit, perhaps. Seeds, thorns. Vegetal things, harvested from the city of the plants. The growing city that existed in stark opposition to the great wasteland of dead buildings out there. That lived, but where human beings could never go.

And then the voice.

It boomed from all around. At first Amri thought it came from the very air. She had no idea what it said; at first she thought it was nothing but monster sounds, because the volume and the accent combined to defeat her. It was loud enough that they would hear it like mad thunder back at the camp, waking with sudden fright to find both her and Guy gone.

Guy tilted his head warily, and his flying machines rose up a little, tilting and veering in the air.

"So you're in there are you, Bruce?"

"It *is* you, is it, mate?" This time she just about understood what the roar of the voice was saying. It wasn't from the sky, but it wasn't from a throat either. There were barrel-bodied plants that were shaking themselves to pieces in sudden mechanical vibration, and from the drumming rattle of them came words. Almost-human words. "You made it down," roared the plant-voice. "Good on you."

"No thanks to you and the others," Guy called back, not quite shouting, but louder than speech, as though talking to a deaf old man. Amri wondered what sensitive leaves or membranes out in the mass of foliage caught his speech and carried it away to whatever existed at the heart of the green.

"Ah, you know how it is," the plant god rumbled, vast and inhuman as conversational weather. "If it hadn't been you, it'd have been you doing it to one of the others."

"Or to you," Guy spat.

"Ah, mate, you reckon you could pull one over on me, is it? Don't think I didn't feel you prying at the cracks in my data security on the way over here. How's that working out for you?"

"So I'm supposed to just nobly accept my defeat, am I?"

"Survival of the fittest, isn't it, mate? Isn't that what we always told ourselves?"

Guy backstepped abruptly, three high prancing motions so that the sudden clench of thorned branches caught only empty air where he had been.

"You're slow, Bruce," he said. "Plants are slow."

"You know what plants are, mate?" the god chuckled genially. "They're fucking *inexorable* is what they are. Right now I'm just gathering resources, taking a bit of a breather after that first big growth phase, but I suggest you look up the meaning of the word 'exponential' in whatever online dictionary you managed to download before we cut you off."

"That's the plan, is it?" Guy demanded. "Just more of this, world without end."

"Oh, I've got about a hundred different biomes planned, mate," the plant god promised hugely. "Algorithmic evolution, procedurally generated species, rewilding the Earth from pole to pole."

"I imagine the others will have something to say about that." Guy made another brisk little move. Amri saw the ground where he had been standing churn and knot.

The fabricated laugh that resounded across the sky was terrifying for its joviality. A pleasant mundane thing bloated out into a nightmare mockery, just like the plants themselves.

"Bug Boy and Plastic Man?" the plant god chuckled. "What's the point of them? We came here to remake the world in our image, Guy. But you all think so *small!*"

Something ripped from the soil before Guy, a curved limb, jagged with thorns. With spring-loaded swiftness it scythed through the air and pulverised the shoots and grass where he'd been standing.

"I'll be seeing you, Guy," the plant god promised, with a parting laugh. "Or at least sensing you. There's nowhere you can hide. No place across the whole world where you can set your feet that I won't know about."

Guy retreated far enough to be out of the green altogether. Amri saw little tendrils spiralling out of the earth where his footprints had been, reaching blindly for something to entangle.

He took a long breath, shook his head. "I know you're there," he called. "Amri, isn't it? I saw you an age ago." He was looking right at her.

"You didn't say anything." She fell into step beside him as he headed back towards the camp.

"I didn't want Bruce to know. I reckoned my being there would hold his attention, and he wouldn't go hunting for any little rabbits."

"Why did you come here?"

"To assess the damage. To collect some samples. He's right, I knew he was coming for me, so I was working on a way to deal with him. Only I was thinking defensively. He just *struck*. And I wasn't ready, not quite. But that doesn't mean the preparations I made are worthless, if I can get myself into a position to use them." He cocked his head, then nodded towards the eastern sky where the first fingers of dawn were showing. "Speaking of which, let's go find some Seagulls."

6.

SEAGULL SHADOWS

Everyone came with them in the end. Remus and Hailfoot and a half-dozen other Rabbits who'd been far enough to outrun that initial burst of predatory growth. All that were left, with nothing to stay for, and none of them wanting to hang around near the creeping boundaries of the green. Especially after Amri had told them what the plant god had said, about gathering strength for another grand push outwards. They formed a ragged cluster around Hailfoot's cart that had been loaded up with all the food and firewood they could find. Hailfoot's boy, and a girl whose straying had made her a live orphan rather than one more among the dead, ranged either side of their path, foraging for berries and mushrooms and bugs, anything they could catch and eat. Everyone else just stared fearfully at Guy's broad back. And at Amri. Because Amri walked at the god's side, and by his reflected radiance had been transformed into something new and strange. And the Rabbit feared new things. In a rabbit's life, almost everything that was not familiar would kill you.

Amri thought about that, and about what had happened anyway. *It isn't enough to fear*, she decided. Fear on its own did not save you. Because the things that you should fear could strike you down anyway. Nobody had legs fast enough to outrun the end of the world. And so maybe being curious about the strange was better because then you could understand it, predict it.

Fight it.

She didn't think the plant god could be fought. The Rabbit told her, *Run, hide. Never fight*. But when she looked at Guy, both those principles blew away, because *he* had a way to defeat even that monstrous growth.

"Will it die?" she asked him.

He cocked an eyebrow at her, and then looked sidelong at the great pseudopod of green to their left. They were travelling alongside the reaching tendril of the plant god's influence as it stretched into the city.

"When you kill the god, will the plants die?" she clarified.

"That," he said, "is an intelligent question." He appeared surprised, but she took it as a victory anyway. Right now it seemed very, very important to make herself a part of Guy's mental landscape, to make him think of her as useful. "It depends," he went on, "on how well Bruce designed them. If they're hothouse flowers, then they'll die off without his intervention, and he was never much interested in the vegetable kingdom before we turned our eyes back home.

But I imagine he built his invasive species well enough to endure. You're thinking of farming them?"

She shrugged. "Maybe."

"I wouldn't. I'd burn the lot. I bet the fruit looks delicious, but you don't know what toxins are in them. At the very least they'll be addictive as hell. He was always one for locking you into brand loyalty. I wouldn't have thought he'd go with getting his hands dirty like a farmer, but I suppose expansion and growth can be physical and not just financial." He gave her a wry glance. "You have no idea what any of this means, do you?"

"Some. How are you going to beat the Seagull?"

"I don't want to beat them. I need to convince them to fight Bruce with me."

"They won't. They're murdering savages. They're no better than he is."

He cocked an eyebrow. "Do you really believe that, though? Because that's small thinking. And when you're up against a big enemy, small thinking will make you lose."

She thought about Beaker and all the stories she'd been told, about the sacrifices, the raids, the casual violence. She wanted Guy to do something godlike and lay waste to the Seagull like the plant god had done with the Rabbit. *Small thinking. Rabbit thinking, not to fight but to hope someone else fights*. She needed to change the way her head worked.

THEY SPENT A night in the ruins. Remus cooked what they had, on the basis that if they wanted to meet the Seagull there was no reason not to light a fire. They didn't come that night, though; off being brutal and vicious somewhere else. Instead Amri lay down near Guy and asked him, after dark, "What was it like?"

"What?"

"You said you went into the sky."

"Into space. To… the next world out from the sun, and then to the moons of further worlds. We built a paradise, Amri. We took the finest minds from Earth—scientists, engineers, artists. We gave them everything they could possibly need, hauled it into orbit and then shipped it out across the solar system. And we built Utopia for them. The four of us, we innovators and leaders, we founded the perfect state. Free of the chains of state control, the short-sightedness, the corruption and backward-looking baggage of it all. It was wonderful. The freedom of expression, the ability to be yourself, without limit. To transcend the limits of Earth."

"To become gods," she translated.

"In a way." As though he hadn't been claiming the title from the start. As though, in his head right then, he was just a man again, as he once had been. Then he caught up and nodded more vigorously. "We were the greatest minds of the world, Amri, we four. United in purpose, back in those days. Knowing that the world was failing, shrinking, becoming too small for our ambitions. And so we did what we could. We took all that was good and lifted it to the heavens. We built a new world to contain and nurture everything worth preserving of Earth. I'll show you how it was. You'll marvel, I promise you."

She nodded. When she reached out to him, she was making a very conscious choice. Because she was like someone clinging to a ledge with her fingernails, and the tiny purchase she had on the world was the fact that she had met Guy. And if Guy wasn't a god anymore, cast out as he had been, he was still an order of magnitude more than anything else around.

He let her hand rest on his chest for a moment, then made a sound, not very surprised. Accepting his due. He rolled over and she felt his hands on her, oddly soft compared to the calloused palms of other men she'd known. The rest happened just as she expected, though. A transaction at a human level, nothing divine about it. She imagined the other Rabbits listening to her, and hoped they were remembering every time they'd scorned and mocked her, back in the godless world of the before. It was a mean thought, but it warmed her. It brought her closer to god.

THE SEAGULL FOUND them midway through the next day. One moment the little rag-train of Rabbits were hauling Hailfoot's cart over a buckled crack in the road, the next there were lean men and women with grey-white feathers in their hair, up on rooftops and leering out of doorways. They had glass-studded clubs and hooked sticks with metal beaks, spears and slings. Ahead, blocking the road as effectively as if he had been an army, was Beaker. From her own rooftop vantage, Amri stared down at him.

Guy made a square between his hands, and she started

back as Beaker's face was suddenly there, shifting about in the air. Every crease and line of him, every smudge and crack on the lenses he wore over his eyes.

"This is their boss man?" Guy asked. He had to ask again before she answered, because the casual magic of it had robbed her of words.

"Their champion," she said. "Probably he could be boss if he wanted. I think the Seagull chief is his brother or uncle or something."

"He'll have to do," Guy decided. The pair of them had left the main group not long before. Guy hadn't said why, but the winged machines had left his shoulders again and she guessed he must have seen the ambush ahead.

He hadn't warned her or the others, but at least he'd taken her with him.

Now Beaker was striding forwards, a spear in one hand and a beaked club in the other. His face jittered out of the space between Guy's hands and then swung back, and she understood that one of the fliers was moving to keep him in its eye.

"What's this?" Beaker demanded—his voice came to Amri faintly from below but clearly from somewhere on Guy's suit. "So many Rabbits in the trap?" She saw his eyes flick left and right. Unaware of the scrutiny, his face told her his every thought, so unguarded as to be indecent. He was suspicious. This wasn't how Rabbits acted. Something was wrong.

Down below, she saw Remus step forward. She hadn't thought he was brave enough, but he was a people person, always the first to go talk to the Pigeon or the Cockroach. Not the Seagull, though, not before now.

"We are all the Rabbit," he told Beaker flatly. "All that is left. Tell me you've not seen what lives where we once lived?"

Amri watched Beaker's face keenly, waiting for the cruelty, the satisfaction that their enemies were dead. Instead, there was something else there, that she'd never have looked for in a Gull.

He has seen. He's afraid.

"All the Rabbit?" Beaker echoed. The other Seagulls were exchanging glances.

"You've seen," Remus said. "The plant god."

"Yes, we've seen." Beaker strode forwards, chest to chest with the man. Not looming physically, but putting Remus in his shadow anyway. "We've seen it not so many streets from here. Is it coming our way to hunt Rabbits, do you think? If we stake you out in its path, will it be happy with your bones?"

"My cue, I think," Guy decided. He put his helmet on, securing it to the neck ring of his suit, and stepped out of cover, up to the jagged brink of their vantage point.

"The plant god isn't here for them," he called.

Beaker stood absolutely still, looking at him, but the other Seagull warriors scattered and then reformed. A single sling-stone struck Guy in the chest and bounced off the plastic plates.

Amri had lost her close view of Beaker's expression, but he held himself still, feet not giving an inch. At his curt signal, the others were moving in on the little band of Rabbits, putting spearpoints before their faces and kicking them back against Hailfoot's cart.

"I like your fancy clothes, Rabbit," Beaker called up, though Amri thought his voice shook a little.

"I am no Rabbit," Guy said. "The gods have returned to the world, Beaker. One stands before you now, and one is out there tearing up the earth in his hunger to get to you. He's not coming for these wretches. What have they got to offer him? He's heard that the Seagull is strong, and he's coming to devour that strength."

And this was nonsense, he'd explained to Amri privately. Bruce the god was coming to the city along the gradient of the land, seeking where the water collected, the concentrations of things that would feed his ever-expanding plant body. The Seagull were incidental. *Correlation and not causation*, he had said.

"Then we'll bring axes," Beaker said. "Come down, god-man. Let us show you how good our axes are."

"Oh, you'll need axes," Guy confirmed. For a moment, despite the disparity of their positions, Amri had a weird sense she'd seen all this before. Two bucks of the Rabbit shouldering and sniping at one another over who was stronger. Two old men shoving each other with words when there was a disagreement around the fire. Just one more slapping match over who was in charge, tiresome in its familiarity.

There were young Gulls scaling the building to either side of them, clambering up with knives in their teeth. Guy didn't seem to notice. "Tell me," he said, "will you bring your axes against this?"

The world dissolved into chaos and horror.

Amri caught a glimpse, just before the transition, of one of the flying machines dipping low. That was all the warning she had. Guy hadn't briefed her about how he would fight the Seagull.

Abruptly they were inside the plant god. Its saw-toothed leaves erupted all around them. Roots boiled up from the ground, coiling in fantastical arabesques or plunging back to earth hard enough to tear apart the city's crumbling concrete. From every crack and wall the fungus grew, white and yellow and phosphorescent green. Vast ribbed fans of it filtered the sunlight into corpse-shades and underwater murk. From that boiling ground she saw the bones of her kin, pierced through with creepers, jolting and rattling like an endless, malign divination. She could hear the screaming of her own people and that of the Seagull. At least one of the climbers must have lost his grip; his cry of terror and the sudden crack of his landing came to her quite distinctly. She clutched at Guy's suit, knowing it was all his doing and yet a slave to her fear even so.

In the midst of it all stood Beaker. Rooted even as the roots grew through him, his eyes still fixed on Guy.

"This is your enemy!" Guy shouted at him. "This and the other gods. They're going to wipe you from the face of the world, to replace you with their own dreams of how life should be. In mere days, where you stand will be swallowed up by the green. It will tear down your homes, strangle your children. I'm showing you your future, Beaker."

Beaker lunged forwards, a single staggering rush that brought him with his maul raised over Remus. "I'll kill your people!" he shouted.

"They're not mine! Kill them all," Guy said calmly. "What will it matter? I am not the god of the Rabbit or the Seagull, or any one clan of you. I am the one god who will fight for the people of the world against my fellows. I'm the one who understands how they can be beaten, the one they tried and failed to kill. This is your one chance to aid me in destroying my brothers, Beaker. Otherwise I'll go find some other people more worthy and leave you to the thorns."

The swirling vision of plant hell around them faded, sinking back into the earth and the walls. In its wake Amri saw her people and the Seagull still cowering, their fear suddenly naked for all to see. Only Beaker stood tall and she wished she could see his face close up again.

He lowered the maul, and then thrust out a hand to Remus. When the man wouldn't take it, he forcibly hauled the Rabbit to his feet. An awkward way to suggest they were all friends now.

"Come down then, fallen god," he said. "Tell us what you want of the Seagull."

7.

VISIONS OF THE MADE WORLD

THE SEAGULL LIVED in rickety gantries all the way up the face of several buildings organised around a square. Amri had never seen it before; why would a Rabbit go to such a place?

In the centre of the square there was a cracked plinth with one bronze foot still showing where some ancient statue had once stood. The Seagull had re-edified it with a great structure of interleaved slats of wood, arranged in two great fans with a projecting metal spar jutting from the centre. If Amri squinted, she could just about see it as some sort of bird. A lot of the wood was studded with little stony knuckles of white and bored with finger's breadth round holes. Later she found the whole thing had been brought upriver when the Gull had been forced to abandon their coastal haunts. It was streaked with white droppings, but then so was the wall beneath every window ledge. The whole place stank of all the worst of birds.

Nobody sacrificed anybody to it while she was there, but she was sure that was its purpose.

She kept close to Guy; the other Rabbits kept close to her. Guy's own attention was on Beaker. The distance between the two men felt like walking a tightrope. Amri kept waiting for the invisible bond to snap and a hundred Seagulls to descend on them with clubs and knives. The rest of the warband Guy had faced down were entirely cowed by what they'd seen, but Beaker still had a glint in his eye that was more than just the sun on his lenses.

He climbed up on the plinth and called out what had happened, how there was an angry god coming to fight them and how Guy had brought the news and come to help, stopping short of calling the man divine. Then he vanished off, presumably to talk to the Seagull's actual leader. The Rabbit clustered in Guy's shadow and countless predatory eyes dissected them. Children threw things, and birds wheeled overhead on white wings like knives, screaming at the world.

Then Beaker came back, pointing at Guy.

"Come, god," he said. "Drink with us. Tell us of your god world." He cuffed a passing boy absently. "These ones, go get them food fit for Rabbits."

Amri was probably intended to be in that second group, but she clamped herself to Guy's elbow like one of the dead shells on the wooden statue, which was how she ended up in a second-storey chamber overlooking the square. The room was draped with cloth of countless faded colours, much of it gnawed by mice and shat on by birds. It smelled of mould and decay, and at least part of that was the woman hunched in a nest of blankets. She was old, her body heavy and her limbs stick-thin. She wore a crown of white feathers interleaved with blue and gold beads, with a bird skull in its centre. The headdress looked uncomfortable. Amri guessed it had been hastily donned to receive their guests.

A fire burned in the chamber's centre, smoke vanishing up through cracks in the concrete ceiling to become someone else's problem. A Seagull child with a white-painted face came with bowls of stew that smelled of fish. Amri determined to have nothing to do with it. Everyone knew that eating fish from the city's river made you mad, or just dead. Except the Seagull, apparently.

Guy lifted his bowl until it clicked against the neck ring of his suit. Amri saw little lights and pictures flicker on the inside, where he could see. He smiled. "Whilst I'm sure the mercury, lead and arsenic levels are the new normal as far as your ecosystem out here goes, there's a whole hell of a lot of digitalis in here, and I doubt you use foxglove as a regular seasoning." He smiled pleasantly, while little telltale flickers chased themselves back and forth about his chin.

Beaker and the Seagull chief exchanged looks, and the old woman shifted painfully, pushing herself more upright. She muttered something and the champion nodded.

"You are a god," he pointed out. "What are such things to you?"

Guy shrugged, and then drained the bowl in one long swallow, before throwing it casually over his shoulder. He stared the pair of them down. "This body," he told them, "is very good. Oh, it's human. It's mine. Just polished up a bit. The new model Man 11.4S. Everyone'll want it. Shame there's only one. I survived the other gods crashing my lander and trashing my terraforming gear. A little light poisoning won't even slow me down."

Only then did Amri quite work out what was going on, and put her own bowl aside hastily. Guy laughed lightly. "Oh, I don't think they salted yours from the same shaker, Amri. Although if I'd just dropped dead I don't imagine you and yours would be having a happy time of it." He looked back at the big Seagull. "They think you cut out people's hearts and feed them to the gulls."

Beaker neither confirmed nor denied it. He wasn't looking furious that the poison hadn't taken, either. Amri was starting to really hate his face, but she had to admire his composure.

"You," Beaker said flatly, "are from the Before. The Made World."

Guy cocked an eyebrow. "Well, I suppose I am. I'm the last survivor of it. Or, me and my fellow gods, but I plan to be the last. Which is lucky for you, as I'm the only one who isn't planning to wipe you off the face of the planet and then forget you ever existed."

The old woman spoke again. Her voice came out throaty and low, mumbled through gums. Beaker listened carefully and nodded again. "Why would they?" he asked, speaking for her. "Why not come as you have, to rule us?"

"Rule? Hardly. Help you, certainly. And they'd do it

because you're less than nothing to them," Guy said idly. "And I don't mean the Seagull, I mean all of you. We assumed everyone was long dead when we returned from paradise. We thought maybe nothing bigger than a bug. It's amazing humans even clung on."

There had been more, but he bit it back, and Amri had known him long enough now to understand he was being tactful. She thought back to what he'd said about the grand venture he and his fellows had left for. They'd taken the best, he said. Which meant those who had been left behind on a dying world had been the worst. Which included her own ancestors, and those of the Seagull, and every other people she'd ever heard of. Small wonder the gods hadn't even considered that such meagre dregs might survive.

"But why come back?" Beaker pressed. "Why remake the world?"

Guy cocked his head, seeming genuinely surprised by the question. "Wouldn't you, if you could?" he asked. He gestured at Beaker's face. "Tell me, you wear those things just for affectation?"

Beaker went still for a moment, reserve cracked and something complex flinching away inside. "They help me read," he said quietly.

If Guy had been surprised by the Seagull's last question, he was positively shocked by this revelation. "*Read?*" he demanded. "You're going to tell me there's an unrotted book left in the whole world? The acid in the paper should have eaten every one of them."

"There is writing," Beaker said. He was oddly defensive about it, as though Guy had caught him out in some perversion. "On stones. Or there is paper copied from paper and copied again. When we came here from the coast, we brought words with us. And more. You are from the Made World. Where the people could create things."

"I am the greatest Maker of the Made World," Guy promised him.

The old woman spoke again, and Beaker jumped to his feet and shouted out of one of the gappy windows.

Moments later a couple of young Seagulls in flapping robes hurried in with... something. It was a big metal box with a see-saw handle on top and cords coming from it. The pair lowered it carefully down beside the old woman. Beaker handed her something: flat, the size of two open hands, dark plastic on one side, cracked glass on the other. The cords were carefully fed into a crack in the object's side, and then the two Seagulls had hold of the handles and were vigorously cranking them up and down.

The glass lit up. First darkly, going from dead black to an expectant living black Amri had never seen before. Then a picture of light appeared. A city. *The* city, Amri felt. Except not a ruin. A great magic kingdom of soaring square towers covered in glass, of spires, of a river only blue-brown. In the sky something metal gleamed, caught in impossible flight.

"The Made World," Beaker said reverently.

"Oh, I know," Guy agreed. "My world. You want it back?"

Behind his lenses, Beaker's eyes went wide. "Back?"

"We returned," the god said, "to restore the world to life. The others have ideas towards that end that don't leave any room for people like you. But I can give you the Made World again. But first we need to beat the others, or else there won't be a world for any of us. Just whichever of them wins out in the end, remaking the world in their tedious image." He reached out for the little lit-up thing. At first Beaker drew it back, but in the end perhaps he considered that Guy had more of a right to the thing than anyone, and handed it over.

Guy ran his gauntleted hands over the back of the device, then pulled the cords out so that the picture died. The two young Seagulls stopped their cranking, breathing heavily.

With absurd theatricality, Guy breathed on the device, though Amri saw his thumbs working too, connecting to some part of the object's underside. The lights glimmered back, and then the image was there again. The city. Then it slid sideways, so smoothly Amri actually looked for it to come sliding out of the edge of the device. In its place on the glass face was a dense landscape of green, seen vertiginously from above. After that, a crowd of people, thousands of them, more than Amri had ever imagined could even exist, waving flags in some form of celebration—or perhaps in war. And then some sort of machines in a vast room: jointed arms and sprays of sparks, and disassembled parts.

"Call your warriors," Guy said. "They tell me the Seagull can fight. Well, you'll need to. But let me lead you, and we'll beat Bruce and his army of trees. I've got a plan. I've got some insider information, from before he did for me up there. But if you want to be part of the future world, Beaker, your people have to work for it."

Beaker remained impassive, leaning back so the old woman could murmur to him. Then he nodded. "We shall put out the call," he agreed. "We shall gather every fighter. It will take some days. They are scattered. Some are watching these gods."

"Good," Guy agreed. "Because that's the other order of business. Why don't you, me and Amri go take a look at the competition?"

8.

COCKROACH DREAMS

She had expected more plants, but Guy told her each god had their own idea how life might be brought back to the Earth. Beaker said what she had thought the first time: that life was still here, built of those pieces that had survived the collapse of the Made World.

Guy shrugged. "If you can call it living," he said, with the air of an old repeated phrase. "You don't think there's a better way?"

The three of them had travelled some way from the Seagull roost. Amri didn't like that Beaker was with them. At first she'd thought he was just there to try to test Guy's godhood again, with knife or cord. After half a day, she reluctantly conceded that Beaker was there because the old world fascinated him. There was something almost childlike in him when he spoke of it, stretched tautly over the hard-man murderer he was.

"All my life," he told Guy now, "I've tried to make things

better. With my hands. With my words. Better for the Seagull. So our children have more than I did and theirs have more than them. That is how the world is made better."

"That's how humans do it," Guy said. "Gods, not so much. If you had the power to just change everything to be better, wouldn't you? Just do it all at once, none of this incremental bullshit."

Neither of them knew the word and he had to explain it, crabbing his hand in short stages like an inchworm. Beaker nodded. "Of course. Who wouldn't?"

"But you have to overwrite everything else. Like all of you—Rabbit, Seagull, everyone else, you're a drawing in the sand. Here come the gods with their big hands, smoothing the sand over so they can draw their own pictures. They're good pictures, of a world that's properly alive again, not this clinging-on you've got going on. But the scratch marks that were *you* are gone. And let's face it, those gods aren't going to take the trouble to just work around your scribbles, add to them, try to make something worthwhile. Way too much work for too little result. Only *I'll* do that."

The stronghold of the next god was looming high above them by then. It had been on the horizon for a while, but Amri had taken it for just another building of the city. It was taller, though, and didn't end in a shattered stump or jagged girders. Instead it was a steep-sided mound. Mostly it was made of earth, glued together by some means she couldn't guess at, but its sides were dotted with other findings: pieces of plastic, metal wheel rims, cloth, skulls. Skulls old and new.

"Who used to live here?" Guy asked. "Which of you people?"

Amri and Beaker both started to say none of their people, then stopped, actually sharing a glance over it. Amri's thought then was, *We are all the same ants, to the gods*, without understanding how apposite the thought was.

"Halfbeak Pigeon over there," Beaker said. "Cockroach there." The mound had been raised at the juncture of the two territories.

"Not anymore," Guy suggested, but then Amri was pointing out a human figure, just walking out in the open at the foot of the mount. Bringing an armful of something, depositing it at the edge of a stream that flowed into the mound. A stream flowing—she squinted—flowing uphill, into the mound. A black snaking channel of…

"Ants?" she asked.

"Figures," Guy said, rolling his eyes. "Ladies and gentlemen, let me introduce you to the god Matthias Fabrey. I assume he's in there somewhere. He has a thing about bugs. Son of a bitch will talk your ear off about how efficient and perfect they are, how they evolved to do all that clever human stuff millions of years ago without ever needing brains for it. Farming, architecture, air conditioning, slavery, all that.

Now she'd seen one, she was spotting the industrious, coursing channels of insects everywhere she looked, bustling in and out of the mound. Guy did the trick with his hands where he brought them a close-up view of the structure itself. It was crawling with individual insects fussing about its surface, in and out of dirt holes and eyesockets.

"Doesn't explain who your man down there is," Guy added. "That's unexpected."

"Cockroach," Beaker decided. "Survive anything."

"Well, let's go have a word and see if he can survive *us*," Guy suggested.

THE COCKROACH WAS a gangling man, bald on top with a long straggle of dark hair falling to the small of his back. He wore a long coat cut from a mosaic of cloth scraps stitched roughly together, and it flapped about his heels when he ran away. The Cockroach had never been fighters. The Rabbit had traded with them sometimes. Probably the Seagull had sacrificed or eaten them, whatever they did with their direct neighbours. Certainly, when Beaker ambushed him in his flight and brought him down, he was properly terrified.

"I didn't!" he squeaked. "I never! Hold off! I'll get it for you!"

A fiery pricking at Amri's ankles turned out to be ants. Just a handful, but when were there ever just a few ants? Beaker bundled the Cockroach up and they retreated further from the mound, and then further still, until whatever life crawled about their feet seemed just the regular lot of the city.

Guy sat back and let Beaker give the Roach a shake, to cement their respective positions. Beaker had seen a lot recently that pushed him way down the pecking order of the world. He obviously appreciated having someone grovelling at his feet.

"You're Iffy, aren't you?"

"If you like. If you say. Iffy, that's me," the Roach agreed desperately. "Ain't done nothing 'gainst the Gull, Beaker. I'd never!"

"What's *that*?" Beaker demanded, pointing to where the mound shadowed the sky, taller than any of the broken stumps of the city.

"That's god, friendo," Iffy said. Amri reckoned his name wasn't Iffy; that was just a name the Seagull put on any Roach they dealt with. "God's come back."

"Come *back*," Guy noted, leaning forwards. "That means he's talked to you."

Iffy took in his suit, his face and accent. "Oh, friendo, what bad trip you spring from? Yes, god talks. We're his devoted worshippers. When he makes the world anew, he lets us live in it. At the edges, like."

"Fucking *Roaches*," Beaker spat, cuffing the man almost absently. "'If you can call it living,' is right," he added. "That's you, is it? Slave to ants?"

Iffy laughed horribly, showing long yellow teeth and ravaged gums. "Oh, friendo," he said, "there's worse things. Ask the Halfbeak Pigeon if there ain't." His long fingers splayed, not towards where Beaker had said the Halfbeak lived, but towards the mound. The patterns of skulls set into the soaring dirt walls. "We see them boiling out of the earth all over. We see them Pigeon go stamping and slapping and setting fires. Like it was a party. Like they was dancing. And the ants! Ants dropping from up top, climbing from below. Ants in the air. Ants and ants and ants. Ants taking every little scrap of flesh and blood and skin off them Halfbeak, man, woman and child. Each scrap on its own, peeled off them, living. Them dancing until there was no meat left on 'em. And we knew it was run, then. Ants no friend to Roaches. But Failboy has a good-mushroom dream. Failboy goes to the mound where they was building, speaks to them ants even as they was driving them stinger in. And the mound speaks back. The man in the mound. The god."

"He's in there, is he?" Guy asked.

"We saw him. Come out his metal house, then the ants build 'round him. In there, sure enough, on account of there's nowhere he can have gotten out of," Iffy confirmed. "But he say he likes us. We're bug people, and he likes bug people. He keeps us 'long as we bring his ants things. Every one of us out, now. Bring heavy stuff the ants'd work a sweat over. Things to eat. Things to build with."

"So what happens when you've stripped the carcase and there's nothing left to bring?" Beaker asked.

Iffy turned that gaunt, long-toothed grin on him. "Then that's all, isn't it? That's the end of the world. But at least we'll have lasted to the very end. Better than the Halfbeak."

Beaker wanted to kill the man, to stop word of them getting back to the god. Guy said the god already knew, or would do as soon as the right ants got back to the nest.

"They got back," came a voice. "I know."

Amri remembered the booming of the vegetal membranes that Bruce Mayall had used to communicate. This was different but akin, a mindless sound repurposed to make human words without tongue or throat. It arose from all around them, a dry stridulation like a thousand whispery husks rustling together and, incidentally, making comprehensible speech.

"That you, Matti?" Guy asked.

"Ah, Guy, my old friend," the whisper whispered back. Unlike Bruce's jovial boom, which had been overflowing with malign character, each of the dry leaf words seemed to arise mindlessly, as though by natural chance. As though they formed sentences by some bizarre and ongoing coincidence, no personality behind them at all. Iffy, who had been partway through sneaking off, paused to listen, eyes wide.

"So you survived what the others did to you," continued the thousand proxies of Matthias Fabrey.

"You're going to tell me you've got clean hands where that's concerned?" Guy asked the air.

"The cleanest. My ants are fastidious," Fabrey responded. "You crashed near where Bruce is building his idiot garden, didn't you? How *is* the old fellow?"

"A smug fucker as usual."

"Ah, well, tell him I'm making a plague of locusts just for him, won't you? Once I've dealt with Padreig."

"Plastic Pat?" Guy said.

"The very same. He and I came down quite close. We're already butting heads. Which is unfortunate for him. I have so many more heads. I'm glad you survived, Guy. I'm glad we had this chance to talk one last time." A breeze seemed to pass through the myriad speakers. Only after did Amri realise it was a sigh. "Now you're out of the running, perhaps we should appoint you as judge. We can build our utopias and you can say who should get to make the world in his own image."

"Who says I'm out of the running?" Guy asked.

"What do you have left?" Fabrey asked. "A few toys. A couple of savages. I don't think you're going to be able to White Saviour yourself out of this one, Guy. I have ten million followers and counting, and they can strip the world bare and rebuild it any way I want. They can spread their wings and let the wind carry them to every continent. They can make new colonies of thousands, starting with a single fertilised queen. Independent reactive hive intelligence under my stewardship. Isn't this the dream, Guy? A workforce that's infinitely loyal and infinitely replaceable and has absolutely no ideas of its own? What we wouldn't have given, back in the old days."

"And yet you're working with the locals. This loser, here." Guy jerked a thumb at Iffy.

"They were," the dry chorus said, "hilarious. Their man, covered in ants, but so hopped up off his head that he just kept telling me how wonderful it all was. Whatever he'd taken, it reacted quite deliciously with formic acid." A rustle of almost-laughter. "Maybe it was the ants bringing samples back to me that convinced me to keep them around. Cockroach people, as though they knew I was coming. Stay out of my way, Guy, and you'll live just a little longer. Go bother Bruce or Padreig. I'll be seeing you, in time. After all, I have so many eyes."

And that, it seemed, was that. The whispers died down

and were gone. Later, Amri found hundreds of dead bugs, somewhere between grasshoppers and ants, a special *talking caste*, Iffy said. The act of Fabrey's speech exhausted them, leaving drifts of the dead; every word fashioned from tiny corpses.

9.

WAR GODS

Guy left the conversation with the insects strangely energised. Even when they saw what the ants themselves were doing, it didn't dent his mood.

To Amri—to Beaker even—it was as bad as, or worse than, the plants the other god was sprouting. At least that seemed a process of growth. The ants had built their mound. Now they were stripping everything from the local area and bringing it to their god. The glittering black roads of their tiny bodies coursed with votive offerings: rodents, birds, lesser insects. There were plenty of shreds and scraps, too—pieces of prey the swarm had overwhelmed and sectioned until what was left was of a scale to be carried by ants. Amri saw a finger, complete with a ring of carved bone. And there were other things: flakes of metal, plastics, pieces of the ancient world, ragged-edged from tiny jaws, deformed from acid.

"He'll break it down," Guy said. "Or the ants will.

Turn it into raw materials that can be used to breed more ants, farm fungus, or be fed to the printers. I think he worked out printing ants. Print-ants? I snuck a look at his schematics before it all went sour between us." He rubbed his hands. "The attraction, to Fabrey, was how much you could get the ants to *do* for you, that you didn't need to think about. Simple machines, but put enough of them together and they do a lot of complicated stuff. It's like, we spent forever studying how insects worked so we could make swarm robots to do stuff. It's how we built a lot of Utopia, because that kind of thing can work really well in low-G." Words, spilling out of him, heedless of whether his audience understood. Or perhaps assuming that, not being gods, they never would. Amri glanced at Beaker, who was frowning, eyes narrow as he tried to follow. *He reads*. She wasn't entirely sure what that even *was*, but it was a thing of the lost days, when humans were mighty and gave rise to gods like Guy Vesten.

"And then," Guy went on, "we worked out what we really needed robot swarms to do, and Bug Boy teaches his actual bugs to be like bots, because that's easier, and they're better at getting on with things without ending up banging their heads against a wall or turning everything into grey goo. Perfect workforce, Matti said. 24/7 and no concept of better pay or conditions."

"He's a god, man," said Iffy, who was still trailing behind them. "That sounds, like, disrespectful."

"Why are you still alive?" Guy asked him. Beaker drew a knife but the god waved him back. "I don't mean it like that, yet. Full points for keen, though." He turned back to Iffy. "Why not just picked bones, cockroach-man? Seriously, just because he thinks you're funny and you carry heavy stuff for him?"

Iffy bared all his long teeth in what might have been a smile, or not. "We like funny. God likes funny." He held up a thumb-sized mushroom plucked from inside his rags. "Need a bit of funny, sometimes."

"This god will come for us too," Beaker noted.

"You can count on it," Guy agreed.

"And you smile."

"Because Matti's already fighting Plastic Pat. That's god number four. You need to remember there was a point all of us saw eye-to-eye—or at least kept our jostling on the covert level. You think how it might be if all three of these clowns were pointed in the same direction. Instead of which…"

The idea was for them to go see where the fourth god had begun to build his kingdom, but before they could get there, a runner from the Seagull found them, a thin girl in a bright plastic tunic, filthy feathers in her white-streaked hair.

"It's come!" she was shouting, even as she pelted down a broken street towards them. "It et the market, Beaker! Everything's gone."

THE PLANT GOD'S next growth phase had come sooner than Guy had thought, sooner than anyone could have believed.

The finger of tentative expansion Bruce Mayall had been extending towards the city had become a terrible green sword tearing into the heart of the place.

The spine of the advance followed a zigzag course where the streets offered a path of least resistance, grass and weeds shouldering aside the tarmac, paving and concrete. Then the solid bones of the invasion followed, the gigantic fungi, the trees, the crushing fists of the briars. A narrow strip of incursion became an arm of impenetrable jungle two blocks wide, every building torn up, every creature strangled and killed.

When Amri and the others got within sight of the river crossing the Seagull had used, the entire tribe was on their side of the water, staring across at what had been their home. It was all green now; green and the colours of the fungi—pallid white, strident orange, bruise-purple. A whole broad strip of city had been pulverised, rewilded with extreme prejudice. The homes of the Seagull were lost within it.

At the water's edge, a great cascade of roots and vines plunged into the river. Amri saw the water around them swirl slowly. A stain was spreading there, the filth-brown colour the river had always been retreating away from something dark, almost blue. She shuddered to imagine being in that water, feeling swift-growing tendrils snare her ankles.

"How soon before it reaches across?" she asked.

"How soon before the next growth spurt?" Guy asked. "I'd thought we had more time honestly. Beaker! Get your chiefs together or however you do it. We're going to need to march right now. You need good heavy axes, fire and inflammables, plus anything you've got that'll poison weeds. You know what I mean?"

Beaker did. Unlike a lot of his kin, he wasn't despairing. Losing his home had just brought out the fight in him that was never far below the surface.

Amri had been checking on her own handful of kin. She'd felt a terrible certainty that the Seagull would have abandoned them, but it turned out the Gull had been more ready to run than the Rabbit, irony of ironies. They remembered losing their coastal haunts to the King Crab. They'd been up and out when the first concrete cracked, and had brought their guest-prisoners with them as a matter of course, just like they'd brought their possessions and their food.

After throwing her arms around Hailfoot and the others, she went and found Guy again, standing at the broken edge of a second storey, watching the Seagull warriors gather. She had a question.

"The world is very big," she said. And that *wasn't* a question, but there was one hiding in it, like a crab in a shell.

"Because by then we'd fallen out," Guy told her. "When we left Utopia we were still saying we were united in purpose but it was obvious everyone had their own plan, and nobody's plan played nicely with others. Aggressive re-greening, making bugs the new feature, the ludicrous nonsense Plastic Pat's up to right now. Fatal compatibility issues, basically. So we knew we'd be butting heads. And we knew that if any of us got left to their own devices without oversight from the others, they'd likely end up with so much momentum that, when the clash finally came, nobody else would be able to stop them. And so—we never agreed this, talked about it, anything like that—but we came down together. On each other's doorsteps. To keep an eye on each other. And to fight. For the future of the world."

And then he was looking down on the troops. Amri hadn't realised the Seagull had so many fighters. There were skinny young men, little more than boys, seamed veterans like Beaker, hard gaunt women and long-limbed girls Amri's own age. There were Seagulls who didn't fight, but they were less than one in three. They had always been a vicious and ugly threat to Amri, and now she looked down on them and saw it had always been true. The fact that they were listening to Guy, therefore nominally on her side, made little difference to it.

Guy had a good voice, or rather his suit took all the self-assurance his voice was full of, and lent it the volume of a shout without straining him. He told them the plant god had come for them just like he said, and that he wouldn't stop until the Seagull were just a mouthful of off-white feathers and bones grown over with roots. But he'd heard they were up for a fight, and he could tell them how to kill even a god if they were brave enough for it.

Amri was watching Beaker's face, mostly. The other fighters were shouting and brandishing their hatchets and machetes, but Beaker was stern and guarded. Not speaking out against Guy, but Amri could read in his face, *If one dead god, why not two?* Afterwards, or after all the invading gods were defeated, Guy would have to watch his back.

"It's basically a matter of attention," Guy explained on the march. "A lot of what Bruce has going is automatic. That's the thing with plants. There's going to be some serious biomechanical defences. Traps, basically. And poisons. But plants aren't exactly good at thinking on the fly, so if Beaker and the Seagull can cause enough havoc, then Bruce has to sit up and take notice. He needs to start pumping a different cocktail into his mycelial network to get the plants to act in new ways that'll put out fires and drive away the pesky little humans. Nothing that'll worry him, but it'll take up some of his mind. His human mind. Because there is a human man in there."

"A human god, like you," Amri clarified. They had been on the road almost two days now, cutting a curving path to give the new spear of green a wide berth.

"Well, you know, less attractive," Guy said with a grin. "And probably less durable, honestly. Given he's always planned to just live in the heart of the vegetable kingdom. But he's in there. None of us were just going to set up something completely autonomous. That's not the point of being a god. The point of being a god is to have the joint running to your specifications. Which means you still need to *be* there, and being there is the point. So we need to get to Bruce, and then mess with him. Which is where you and me come in."

Amri blinked at him. "Me?"

Guy shrugged. "Sure. You want revenge on Vegemate for eating your people, right? I'm giving it to you. Call it a present."

Amri just stared at him. The Rabbit didn't do revenge. True, there hadn't ever been anything on this scale to seek revenge *for*, but even so.

Guy frowned, the first time she'd ever seen him uncertain. "Look, I need someone on this that I can trust," he told her. "You've got what it takes, I know you do. I've always been able to look at a potential employee and know what I can rely on them for. You're exactly what I need here."

"Can't you—?"

"I can't, because the other part of Operation Distraction is when I turn up in the middle of Bruce's farmstead, because if there's one damn thing the fucker will fixate on, it's me. He did his best to kill me on the way down, after all. Unfinished business is a bitch. But that means I need someone for some stealth work, Amri. And who else have I got? These Seagull clowns aren't exactly subtle, and I need Beaker to keep them pointed in the right direction. So it's you, basically." He clapped her on the shoulder. "Tell me I can rely on you."

In the face of that divine confidence, who could say no?

10.

ROOT AND BRANCH

T̲h̲e̲ S̲e̲a̲g̲u̲l̲l̲ h̲a̲d̲ wanted to fight the plant god at the site of their own village, but Guy had said they'd achieve nothing. "Like cutting at someone's fingernails in a fight," were his words. Beaker's expression suggested he'd won fights that way, but Guy told them flatly, "We need to get to the heart. Where Bruce is. We could cut and burn and poison for a week, and the next burst of growth would undo everything." So here they were, back at the beginning.

She couldn't even recognise the hill in there, so voracious was the plant life. Nothing of the Rabbit remained save her and the little trailing handful who were now carrying the spare weapons of the Seagull and drawing their carts. Making themselves slaves and servants, because it was that or be abandoned to the cruel world.

She'd been quite untouched, seeing the Seagull muster, brandishing their chopping blades, their clay pots with the oil-dipped wicks, even the big bellows-and-pole contraptions Beaker claimed to have invented that could throw a spray of flaming jelly twenty feet. That had just been noise. Then she'd understood that the vastly overgrown terrain ahead was All She Had Ever Known, even if she'd only lived at the very periphery of it, and something new had come to live in her.

"I want revenge," she told Guy. The words felt spicy and sharp in her mouth, like ground glass mixed with pepper. They were not Rabbit words. She had learned them from a god.

He grinned at her, boyish in his enthusiasm. She had to remind herself that he was many lifetimes old. "You'll have it. Bruce is going to have a very bad day, and serve the fucker right for messing with me. Although I'll give the Gull their due, they'd have put up a fight before they went down. Fucking *flamethrowers*. Hey, Beaker!" And when the man came over, strapping on a bandolier of what Guy called 'Molotoffs': "Your name's a good one. Back in the day, it was a science thing, not just the pokey end of a bird."

Beaker regarded him without expression and then said, "That is why I chose it for myself. The science man. We found moving images on one of the mirrors that worked. The blind bald man with these," touching the rims of his lenses, "who knew science, he gave a name to my teacher. I was the other, the tall man with the fiery hair who endured the science. Then my teacher died, and I became the one who knew science."

Guy stared at him, and for a brief moment he wasn't a god, just a baffled, incredulous man. Then he shrugged. "You'll have to show me sometime."

"That one is lost. But we have others. We have seen the golden age." He glanced at the wall of plants, at the warriors psyching themselves for the fight. "You are a man from that age. Perhaps that makes you a god. But will you bring it back?"

"There were many men back then. They weren't gods," Guy told him. "I made myself a god through my vision. I was great enough to build a new world when the old one was failing. We all were. We had vision."

"Like that?" Beaker indicated the predatory forest with a tilt of his head.

"It's *a* vision. Just be glad it's not mine."

For a moment the two of them glowered at one another, then Beaker backed down. "We start burning now?" he asked.

"Go do that voodoo," Guy agreed obscurely. When the Seagull champion had gone to shout at his squabbling flock, he turned to Amri. "Rabbits don't mind enclosed spaces, I'm thinking?"

"My drones found the entrance," he told her. "I know you call the inner bit by the river 'the city,' but this was *all* city, and it's connected by transport tunnels that run under it. There's an entrance in there, where Bruce is. Right near your village."

She nodded. They'd had it ready to retreat into, if the village had been attacked. Not that it had helped in the end.

They were standing at a rubble-choked hole that

nonetheless had just enough room to squeeze into. Below was stagnant water, seething with the crooked thumbs of mosquito larvae and the blind fish that fed on them. Amri had caught both in her day, but there would be rats too, and maybe feral dogs.

None of them wanted to go near Guy. When they descended—when the yelling started up above—the water boiled with every living thing trying to get away from him. "Ultrasonics," he said, as though it was a magic word. By then Amri understood he just meant some knowledge from his own day or his own genius for invention that gave him control over the world. That was the heart of godhood, she understood. Knowledge and command, that turned a man, even a man of centuries like Guy, into a god.

Up above, Beaker's people would be attacking. The sounds of fighting were eclipsed swiftly by the echoes of water and breath in the tunnels as she and Guy waded and clambered there. The water stank, and she knew it was poison save when rains had flushed it clean.

The ancient tunnels had arched roofs. Guy's machines supplied a flat grey light, and she saw a hanging garden of metal wires and struts that had once run like a ribbed spine straight down the centre but now hung in disarray. An inverted forest of hungry roots had cracked the ceiling in a hundred places, many hanging down to dabble in the water. Without needing to be told, she avoided them. They were the advance sentries of the plant god. If she touched them, surely a signal would boil back up the tendrils until it reached their master.

She wondered how the Seagull were getting on, with their incendiaries and fire arrows and blades. She realised she wasn't sure what she felt about them now. They were her enemies, and she should want them and the plant god to worry each other to mutual destruction, but those thoughts belonged to a woman who still had a people. She just had a god.

"They'll die, a lot of them," Guy said. At her startled glance, he added, "You keep looking up. I mean, they're not actually *up*, because they'll still be chewing at the edges of things and we're pushing inwards down here. But I assume that's what you're thinking. They'll die, but they'll cause enough damage for our purposes. And this is in their best interests. That's what everyone always forgot, when things got tough. Sometimes the future demands sacrifice. Hard work, privation."

His flying shoulder machines had found something. "Our way up," Guy confirmed. "Now, what you and the Seagull both get to be glad about is that Bruce and I were already fixing for a fight before anyone arrived back on Earth. We all four of us knew how things would go, and we were looking for ways to sabotage each other. I'd got into Bruce's plans, but it turned out he was in mine as well. He didn't even let me touch down before he screwed me over. But, because he couldn't even get that right, here I am with enough understanding of his set-up here to return the favour. Now I'm going to go up and engage the son of a bitch in conversation, give him a chance for his supervillain monologue. *You* need *this*—"

He pressed a chain of little plastic containers into her hands, the last of them still feeding out of the machines in his suit.

"There's going to be a big old gourd up there, in the middle of it all," he said. "It's a life support system." Looking at her doubtfully. "Like a house Bruce lives in. House and servant all in one. Keeps him safe and fed and connected to the big plant organism-ecosystem he's got going up there. I'm going to send a drone with you, and it'll target areas you need to apply these to, while Bruce is venting on me, okay?"

She nodded. What else was there? Then they had reached where the drone was circling and she saw what it was illuminating.

This was indeed the entrance to the underworld that her village had been built around. Where her people had planned to flee in times of trouble. And trouble had come and they had tried to flee.

The way up was blocked by a grotesque plug that was roots and bodies and obscene outgrowths of fungus, all clenched into a single bolus of biological matter. The smell hadn't forewarned her because the stagnant water's own stink just gradated into it, one foulness welcoming the company of another.

Amri made a noise. Guy glanced at her. For a second his face was blank, unable to understand her upset. Then some deliberate part of him caught up and he mummed sympathy, but she wouldn't ever forget that moment of disconnect, when she was a misbehaving thing and not a person.

"Give me one of those." When she didn't move, he took a little canister from the belt he'd given her. "Amri—Focus, Amri! Watch. This is how it's done. But you've got to be ready to move, because when I do this, all hell's going to break loose."

She nodded convulsively without actually being sure she could move any closer to the horror the drones' lights showed her. She was fighting to avoid looking for faces, actually grateful of the accelerated decay, the merciful shroud of corruption that blurred all details.

Guy selected a root and jammed one canister end against it. She heard a click, and when he removed it, a metal needle stood proud, still dripping where it had gone in.

The root shuddered. She expected it to recoil, lash about like a serpent. Instead it bloated out abruptly, the white inner flesh forcing apart the bark. Something burst with a retort like green wood snapping on a fire. Guy stepped back, expressionless.

"Just enzymes, really," he said. "I didn't even have to invent them. Bruce needed something to dissolve away elements of his own structure he didn't need, because that's necessary for growth. Only, if you synthesise a massive concentration of them and inject it at the right point, the resultant dissolution destroys vital infrastructure and... things start to come apart."

Things started to come apart. The root shattered under the force of its own internal struggle, and then another went the same way. Amri understood that it wasn't just about the point that these *enzymes* had been injected, but where that connected to, and where it went next. The insides of creatures were like these tunnels, a network of connections, one part to another. So it was with Bruce's plants. And now the whole hideous glut of matter above was shuddering and rotting.

It shifted, and she saw what would happen and wanted none of it. Guy had her arm, though. She saw his lips move, and probably he was shouting, "Ready?" but then it all came down. The roots, the bodies, the rot, all of it losing its cohesion, sliding and slithering apart into terrible, recognisable fragments, thundering into the water and washing towards them. And Guy, instead of fleeing like any sane man, was pushing forwards like a god. Pushing, clambering, finding the steps that led upwards and powering on towards the sun.

She snapped, her mind a blank, twisting from his grip out of sheer horror. *Run* said Rabbit, but by that point the flood of slimy, half-digested pieces was all around. To go with its flow would be to prolong her time in its company. And so her blind panic had her scrabbling forwards, pawing through the mulchy softness of decay, clawing at disintegrating roots, until abruptly the sun was on her face and she saw the plant god in all his glory.

11.

MAN VERSUS WILD

They were in the heart of her village, but there was nothing left. Every hut was torn apart and overgrown, as though a thousand years had passed. Every field was a verdant explosion of simultaneous growth and decay. She could watch the plants reaching upwards, opening to the sun. Spotting, wilting, furring with mould and returning to the mulch of decay that underlaid it all. That sucked at her feet and thickened the air with the legume stench of vegetative decomposition.

And ahead, through a tangled screen of vines, a great gourd the size of four houses together, its curved walls greenishly translucent. Within, she could dimly glimpse a humanoid form, out of all proportion, bloated and swollen, ten feet tall at least. It hung there in whatever dense medium filled the gourd, arms moving in sweeps and lunges. Coils of intestine or vine or cable pierced it in a dozen places, leading in sluggish loops to a clenched knot she could just make out in the floor below.

The figure flailed abruptly, and she saw that hazy head cast blindly about within its sanctuary.

"Guy?" The plant god's voice boomed from all around them, membranes and hollow trunks resounding with it. "It *is* you, you durable little grub. This is your new Utopia, is it? Playing *Dances With Wolves* with these inconvenient locals?"

Guy stepped carefully away from the pit they'd crawled up through. She saw his feet come down on tendrils and creepers that recoiled from the pressure—not the animal motion of something stepped on, but the mechanical spring of tension released. *Telling the god where he is*, she understood, seeing him carefully selecting where to tread.

"Well, if I hadn't, I'd probably be dead by now, and then we wouldn't have a chance to have this chat," he addressed the air. With one hand he signalled Amri to go forwards. One of his owl-silent drones ghosted past her, projecting red lines of light forwards. *Step here, and here*. A dotted line leading her to the gourd.

And the god would see her, surely. She could not just hide behind the great stalks of greenery, the crinkled fans and shelves and caps of the fungus, because all that *was* the god. How could the trees not see her for the wood? Except, while plants knew the sun, and turned to it, what did they *see?* What information was being fed to Bruce within his pod? A battery of senses beyond anything she could imagine, but not sight.

She stepped and stepped, following the drone, even as the gods sparred with words.

"I'm killing them, you know," Bruce boomed conversationally. "Your deforesting squad. They're tenacious little bastards, I'll give you that. By thorn and branch, irritant pollen, acids, spines and traps I'm getting them. I've let them get some way in, the peskiest of them. Closed the way behind them. I can wait, and they'll keep longer that way. You've brought me a whole consignment of nitrogen-rich fertiliser, Guy. That was considerate of you."

"I knew they weren't going to just slash-and-burn all the way to you," Guy said. "But they're giving me a chance to make my pitch." He gestured at Amri again, clearly saying, *Hurry up.* Around him, plants were growing and spreading, moving the only way that plants can, closing in.

"Is that right?" the plant god rumbled speculatively. "You setting yourself up as a barbarian employment agency these days? Going to offer to lead your sad little Conans against Pat and Matt for me?"

"Why not?" Guy asked, and Amri was next to the gourd, crouched beneath the swell of its side, cowering from the vast, misshapen form within. She had the first canister in hand and the drone showed her where to apply it. A sudden jab at a bulbous knot of roots at the gourd's base. She flinched, waited. Nothing happened. No sudden rot, no uncontrolled growth.

It hasn't worked. But the drone was circling around the gourd's circumference, mindlessly bringing her to the next point.

"I'd have said it was beneath you," the plant god mused, "to actually make *use* of this vermin. What happened to a pristine, clean world for us to reshape? You should have killed them off."

"Now or later, what's the difference?" Guy said. "But right now, I'm a free agent. Sure, my own plans are screwed, thanks to you, but you've got the other two to deal with. I know you've been working on your own plans for them. So let me help."

"Saint Paul to my Green Jesus, is it? Bringing the good news?" Bruce asked. "Hey Pat, you hear that? He doesn't like you anymore."

A net of strangling vines that had been invisible in the foliage above suddenly dropped into view, as did the body it contained. Amri let out a squeak of horror, clapped her hand to her mouth, waited. As promised, though, Guy had the god's full attention. She injected the second cannister, glancing to see if the first had begun some slow-acting assault. Nothing. She tried to catch Guy's eye, but he was staring at the corpse.

Not a corpse. It still moved, and at the same time it was plainly not alive. Amri stared, so that the drone had to nudge her to make her move on. Where she had been, she saw crushed leaves and the pale worms of roots, sluggishly exploring the dents left by knees and feet. Above her, the plant god's indistinct form shifted suspiciously.

The thing in the net was made of plastic, but the only reason she knew was that the grip of the plants had ruptured it, torn the integument of its skin, exposed white joints and the clear, rubbery stuff of its musculature. An artificial person with a blank, out-of-focus face which abruptly sprang into motion, eyes rolling towards Guy. The lips moved, out of sync with the tinny, crackling words. "Is that Guy you have?"

"Padreig?" Guy asked.

"Technically you're seeing a prototype ambassador model." A jag of static that sounded like a snickering laugh. "There has been a breakdown of diplomacy."

"Pat wanted me to lay off while he stamped on Matti," the omnipresent voice of the plant god explained. "Said, 'Let's finish this like gentlemen.' You know what I said?"

"You said screw him," Guy supplied. He was moving now, like a man trying to find his way out of an invisible maze, finding walls every way he turned. Amri injected another cannister, and then the next, and nothing. And now she only had one left.

"I said screw him," Bruce confirmed. "And screw you too. I need none of you. I'm not just remaking the world, mate, I *am* the world. I will be the whole world, and the world will be me. It's just like we all dreamed."

"Not me," Guy said.

"Oh, I'm sure you told your primitives that you were the good guy, Guy. The only good god. But I know what you'd have done with the place if you'd only had the chance. It's better this way. Let it all go back to nature, and by nature I mean *me*."

Amri had paused, and Guy gestured at her furiously. Then the trap snapped on him. Abruptly a dozen saw-edged vines that had been wound tight with tension were released, and he was caught, strangling in their embrace. Amri saw the thorns of them score pale lines in his suit, the tips whip and coil and dig into every soft part they could find.

"You're making a sequence of escalating mistakes," said the erratic voice of the plastic ambassador.

"I never liked you," Bruce said. "I never liked any of you." And then: "Who's this?" And Amri realised her time was up.

Without warning there were thorns driving from the muck around her, filthy with decay, hollow, barbed. They curved for her, cued by every footfall. She felt the ground beneath her boil with sudden expansion, making her stumble. The drone was swatted away by a sudden eruption of fungus.

But she had been paying attention to the structures it had led her to. Now she saw the last one, already half-concealed by a spreading fan of hard, glossy leaves. She lunged for it, feeling their edges cut like glass. Forced her bloody hands into the closing gap and rammed the cannister home.

For what it was worth.

"Pathetic," Bruce said. "You have a pet. We left them *behind*, Guy. We left them because they were too stupid to share our vision. And they didn't even have the common decency to die. Better all trace of them is wiped away."

"We will preserve—" the ambassador started, and then the vines clenched and it was abruptly in pieces, inorganic fluids jetting from its broken joints.

"And now you," Bruce said.

And then the tissues at the foot of the gourd puffed out, abruptly filling with fluid, swelling, bursting with wet pops.

"What?" Bruce demanded. "What? You son of a bitch, what did you do? There is goddamn *nothing* you can brew that can get through to me. I'll have this—have this put down in a—"

"It's not from me," Guy said tightly. The vines were about his neck and his one free hand was hauling at them, fighting for a half-inch of breathing space. "It's your own. I copied it over on the way down. It's just what you use to clear old growth for new. Concentrated. A hundred times. Drown in your own decay, you plant bastard."

Bruce roared. Amri thought he was still trying to speak, but only raw sound resounded from the plants around them. She saw each node she'd injected swell and burst in a spatter of rot, the whole root system that fed the gourd abruptly black and dying. And within, the huge form of the god-man was thrashing, fighting, clawing at the thickening medium. The liquid swirled sickly yellow and became opaque, and she felt the sides shake and tremble with the struggle going on within.

For a moment he was there: a bloated hand pressed palely to the inside of the gourd, a deformed face with one rolling eye. His jaws worked as though he was trying to *chew* through the tough rind and be born again. The sight was too horrific even for screaming. She just stared, witnessing the death agonies of a god.

After, Guy came and laid a hand on her shoulder, lifted her up. She had expected the whole vast vegetable kingdom to collapse, a circle of death spreading out from the gourd, but it lived still. The new world of gods and monsters wouldn't bring her village and her life back to her.

Something had gone out of it though, as was only fitting. The genius loci of the forest was dead, the plants were just plants. What further growth and decay they brought would be on a mortal scale, controllable and comprehensible. A strange realisation, unexpectedly solemn, that something had gone out of the world that could never be restored to it.

"Brutal." The voice from the severed head of the plastic ambassador. It was faint, and fading. Greasy fluid leaked from the ducts of the thing's neck. "Come and chat, Guy. When you're in the area. You'll find me more reasonable than Bruce. You're living in diminished circumstances right now, but I can preserve you."

"I'm sure," said Guy, and then kicked the head savagely off into the trees. "Let's go see how the Seagull's doing," he said to Amri.

12.

THE MIRROR OF THE MADE WORLD

"When we killed the Rat and drove them from the riverbanks," Beaker said, "some we kept, to work, to earn their place. Some we cut the heads from, and the heads went on poles, and the birds feasted. Seagull asks little, gives less, but trophies he likes."

Amri nodded. The two of them were sitting in the ragged hole where two windows had once been in a second storey wall. Below, the Seagull people were engaged in something partway between a celebration and a wake. Above, at the highest point the sloping collapse of the roof allowed, was Guy.

"Heads," she echoed. Probably showing interest now would be a useful survival trait for later, when the Seagull tried to test Guy's divinity. Right now, he was their hero though. He'd delivered exactly what he promised. The plant god was dead. And though Beaker had hacked open the gourd, disgorging a vile curdled slime and the foulest smell

Amri had ever been near, he hadn't taken Bruce's head. The thing that had slithered bonelessly out had been just about recognisable as a human body, but it began deliquescing the moment it met the air, like some short-lived mushroom. No trophy for the Seagull. They weren't about to stick pumpkins and yams up on spikes for the birds, after all.

Below was where the Seagull village had been. They'd hacked a path to it through foliage where the worst danger was spraining an ankle tripping over the roots. Their buildings were partly torn down, partly overgrown. The Gull had started clearing everything then lost interest. Now, they were apparently happy to live in a grove in the heart of the city, especially when the water that Bruce's roots had grown into and weirdly transmuted proved sweet and fresh. A blessing from the god they'd killed, and probably that made sense if you were a Seagull.

They'd taken everything they'd cut down and built a fire, now throwing a plume of white smoke high into the sky. That was also significant, she understood. You wanted your wake-fire to be seen by other tribes, so they didn't forget you were out there. Around it, on pallets, were the dead. Thirty-three of them, bravos of the Seagull strangled by vines, carved up by saw-edged leaves that had suddenly snapped on them. Suffocated by spores that triggered fatal allergic reactions and closed their throats. Poisoned by thorns. One surviving building was serving as the infirmary for the forty-one more still dying of the poisons the plant god had deployed against them. Counting both sides of the life-death border, the Seagull had lost a third of their fighting strength. Yet they whooped and drank and danced. Joyously, she'd thought at first; now, watching those fevered eyes, the shaking hands, she understood it was desperately. Trying to wrest back control of the future from the vast forces that had come to upend their world. Not so different from her own people, in the end. Save that the Gulls *had* fought, even against a god.

"You don't like us, little Rabbit," Beaker needled. "You are the priestess of the good god and you will poison his ear about us." He was grinning, as though he was rested now and more than ready to go up against another divine entity.

"Don't call me that," Amri said.

Beaker blinked. "Priestess?"

"Rabbit. There is no Rabbit."

"Then what are you?"

"Amri Alone." And down there, too, were others, Hailfoot and the rest, and doubtless they still clung to the sad little scraps of fur the Rabbit had left behind, but she realised that she was too far from them now. Closer to Beaker than to those who'd grudgingly consented to call her kin. The gods had changed her.

Beaker's eyes appraised her, lenses making them shift and glitter. "Is that so," was all he said, but without mockery. He hoisted himself up, about to slip down and join the others. "If you speak to the good god"—and *there* was a title spoken with mockery—"ask if he has found a cure for the toxins yet."

* * *

IT WAS WHAT Guy had said he would try to discover. She knew he wasn't doing it.

"I'm surprised you care," he remarked, when she'd climbed up to him and spoken about it.

"Who says I care?" She shrugged. "I said I'd say it, and now it's said. You're fighting the other gods, in your head."

He nodded, shook his head, shrugged so that the machines roosting on his shoulders rustled their filmy wings. "I'm working through Bruce's cache." His expression saying he knew she wouldn't understand.

"His weapons against them," she translated.

His smile was approving. "Okay, fine. Yes. Because we were all tooling up, on the way in. We all had our spies in the others' houses. Electronic, virtual, but spies nonetheless. I'd worked out what Bruce and Matti and Padreig were going to do to the place. I could see there was no room for me in those plans, but just as importantly there wasn't any room for each other, either. Mutually exclusive, this town isn't big enough, et cetera.

"So I was already raiding Bruce's greenfinger library for something that would screw him over. Something that was *his*, so that he wouldn't just register it as foreign and shut it out. And you saw how that went. And Bruce didn't even wait for me to get down, of course. He sabotaged my lander, and bad luck to him my body and my suit were designed beyond all reasonable tolerance so that I came down hale and well, just stripped of all my…"— he glanced at her—"godlike power." A self-deprecating grin she didn't quite believe. There were hollow spaces behind the words he used, things unsaid whose echo she could still hear.

That might be her problem or it might not. And what she was about to put to him might be his problem or just hers. A lot depended on just how godly Guy actually was right at this moment. Superhuman, certainly. Bigger and stronger, and filled with a great mouldering hoard of things he knew that nobody else could. She didn't know if it would save him from a knife in the eye.

If Guy fell, she'd fall too, she had no doubt. His reflected radiance let her walk in safety amongst the Seagull, such as she'd never thought possible. Even Beaker was wary of her. But it was borrowed robes only. Right now, until she found some new guardian to replace Rabbit, Guy was all she had.

"You need to go impress them," she said flatly. "Or leave. Right now you have them, but the Seagull's no tame bird. Not like the Roach with their bug god. They'll test you. Win them, or leave."

"I may have to kill Beaker," he said. Not quite a non-sequitur. "But also, he's useful. He knows things. I'd rather have him as a lieutenant who can get things done without being spoon-fed. So maybe you're right. Time to unveil my vision, I guess."

He went down, picking his way through the twisted snarls of lianas and the surviving concrete steps and blocks until he was below, amongst the Seagull. Talking to the old woman who led them, to Beaker, to others who seemed important. Until he had them hang pale cloth over the most intact of the surviving walls. He stood before the impromptu screen, his suit amplifying his voice until the echoes came back twisted from buildings streets away.

"The gods have returned to your world!" he boomed. The artificial resonance reminded Amri unpleasantly of the way Bruce had spoken, before he died. Guy was in his element, though, pacing before them, his neck-ring display lighting up his face. "Well, you knew that," he said. "We killed one today."

Some cheers.

"Bruce dreamed of a green world. There are worse things. Except his world had no room for anyone else in it. Nothing but Bruce, equator to poles, land and sea. So he had to go, and now he's gone. The other two are worse. One of them wants to cover the world in ants. The other wants to—well, if Plastic Pat gets his way, it won't just be us who's dead. It'll be everyone and everything. And tomorrow I'll go take a look at how he's getting on with that.

"But we'll stop them. We'll stop them both like we stopped Bruce. Because I'm the god who kills gods. I'm the god who remembers how it was back in the day. And I'm bringing the day back."

Perfect timing: the screens lit up with a sunrise more glorious than any Amri had ever seen. And she knew it was just the drones projecting images, but that didn't mean her breath didn't catch. The part of her that knew couldn't override the part that felt wonder.

And then the vision had escaped the screen, so that all that work hanging everything up was just misdirection, a trick to point people in the right direction because the city was coming back to life around them. The fallen buildings made whole, first around them, then expanding further out. Tall silver towers flashing in the gleam of that unreal dawn, spires topped with winking lights, building after building flashing into impossible completion as the Seagull gasped in awe.

"Alone of the gods, I come to lead you back to that golden age," he told them. "You've shown me you can fight. You've shown me you're worthy." Now there were flying machines up there, above even the sky-reaching towers. Silver crosses passing overhead with ponderous dignity so that her ears ached for the roar of them. "If you'll follow me," said Guy. "If you'll let me."

And when she moved, it was all wrong. When she turned her head away from that set direction, the proportions of everything fell apart and the illusion was lost. He hadn't reconstituted those far buildings, or even projected images onto them. It was all a trick of perspective, good for one angle only. But it was enough to win the minds of the Seagull. Doubtless they saw themselves as the elite in those mirror-walled towers, and didn't ask who lived in the unseen darkness of the streets below.

Or not all, perhaps. Later, towards the real and unspectacular dawn, Beaker came to find her again. He had the little mirror he'd shown her, that still glowed with power ever since Guy had touched it.

"Let me show you a thing," he told her, and began moving pictures about its little glowing screen.

"What is this?"

"The mirror remembers a little of the old world," Beaker said. "Only a little. Because in those days there was an... invisible marketplace, and library, and fighting ring. And the people of those days said, why do we need these libraries and this learning with us, when it is in the marketplace and our things can go there for us at any time and fetch them. Except now here is the thing, but there is no marketplace. The talk that happened there between people, and the knowledge that was in their stalls, all of it gone. So we have only what is within the mirror, and has survived the years."

"How do you know all this?" Amri challenged him. Beaker the murderer was someone she felt she could step carefully around. Beaker the *scholar* and murderer was like a beast all the more dangerous because she couldn't know quite where it was in the darkness.

"From the mirror. From others. From writings. The good god, the Guy, he has more of a name, that he's told you." And a gap that the end of the sentence fell into. A gap she couldn't see into, containing the shape of just where she and Beaker stood with one another.

"Why?"

"Because I will ask the mirror about him. And then you and I can both see what it knows." Half of a peace offering, half of a conspiracy.

"Vesten," she said, the name surfacing, though she

couldn't have recalled it for her life a moment before. "Guy Vesten." Hushed, as though saying it would summon him.

Beaker spent a moment puzzling over that, trying to code the word into the sounds, then into the letters that would conjure results from the mirror. Then there was a familiar face on the screen, and again, repeated over and over. Guy, thinner, wearing the formal, confining clothes of the old days. Beaker squinted at the tiny characters on the cracked screen, selected this image or that, brought up more pictures. One was Guy with three other men, and though none of the faces were familiar, there was a weird commonality to them. Not the features but the expressions, the lordliness of them, the implicit superiority over whoever might see the picture. *The gods*, she knew. She decided the meatiest of them was Bruce, the dead god. The one with the weirdly smooth face, like he was already transforming into his own divine avatar, was Padreig, which meant the angular man with the eyeglasses like Beaker's must be Matthias Fabrey, he of the insects.

"It talks about them going," Beaker said. He was peering carefully at the marks beneath the picture, his lips moving with the effort of it. "Building Utopia, like the god said." And then selecting a word set in another colour, swapping one picture for another. There was Guy standing at the centre of a group of men and women, some in white, others in orange, a few in armoured suits like the one Guy wore now. Everyone seemed very happy, but none as happy as Guy. But why shouldn't they be happy? As Beaker revealed, they were leaving the world to go make Utopia. A new future for humanity, freedom and opportunity, the brightest minds working together under the guidance of none other than entrepreneur and tech-genius Guy Vesten.

She stared at all those faces, the smiles with a hint of strain behind them, and thought.

13.

IN THEIR MILLIONS

THE ANTS ARRIVED before the dawn did and nobody was ready. Amri was curled up with Hailfoot and the other ex-Rabbits on a rooftop, waking sporadically because the Seagull were still celebrating their great victory. Laughter, whoops, cheers. Cries, yells of alarm, screams. The one blended into the other in the shallow layer of her dreams and she didn't immediately understand they were under attack because screaming and the Seagull were inextricably linked in her head.

Then Remus was shaking her awake. She sat up to see a bright blaze running up the side of the building across from her—cloth hangings alight and consuming themselves even as she watched. The fire misled her as to what was happening. She spent too long thinking of water, thinking that, up on this uneven concrete stub, they would be safe.

Down below, the Seagull were running back and forth, stamping at the ground, scratching at themselves. She saw one old man fall and writhe on the ground, flailing and clawing at his face as though he was possessed. Everyone acted as though an enemy army was within their camp, and yet there was nothing, nobody. Just shadows and smoke from the fires.

Something jabbed her bare foot, like a tiny needle of glass. She yelped and saw the ant. Just an ant, a large one, enough to pierce her skin with its jaws and stinger, but one ant. Who would ever be frightened of one ant?

Looking over the edge, then. Recontextualising the flurries of darkness that moved across the ground like the shade cast by clouds scudding over the sun, save that it was night.

Ants.

The creations of the plant god had been vast; the great earthen tower of the insect god had been vast too, but *big* wasn't the only weapon a god could use to rid the earth of inconveniences. Sometimes *small* worked too.

The first flier blew past her, filmy wings flurrying at her face before the breeze carried it away. Looking to the quarter where the insect god's tower was, she saw a boiling cloud eclipsing the stars.

They ran. The rooftops, where they could. Jumping gaps and hauling one another over the broken teeth of fallen walls. A sudden vertiginous shift of perspective, seeing the city around them like a vast boneyard of the ancient days, and she and Hailfoot's boy and all the others just insects themselves. No more than ants devoured by ants, devoid of significance. Matthias Fabrey's hive would live on, and that was all that mattered.

Hailfoot had seen where the Seagull were going. A column of them, their children, their aged, funnelling out of the camp and onto the river. Boats and rafts and planks, in the hope the water would stand as a barrier to the ants. And Amri wouldn't have wanted to trust that contaminated flood against her skin, save that the plant god's clutching roots had cleansed it perhaps just enough. Between the Rabbit and the riverbank there was a jigsaw of shattered buildings rising out of a ground seething with dark bodies already picking the last shreds of sustenance from bones. Rising like a tide up the scarred brick and cement.

Remus had torches, rags wrapped around sticks, lit from the fires already raging—anti-insect measures that had escaped their makers' control. They forged towards the water, leaping from high ground to high ground, thrusting flames at the swelling advance of the tiny attackers whenever they had to dip lower.

"The god!" Hailfoot's boy shouted. "Guy! Good god! Save us!"

Amri looked around wildly. Across from them, on another rooftop, there was Guy. He was just regarding the steadily encroaching tide, and she could read nothing in him. Not despair, not contempt, nor that he had a plan. And he hadn't mentioned any of this the previous night, no warning to the Seagull that their next divine foe would be on them before the dawn. The ants had stolen a march on him. Whatever measures he'd been planning to deal with Fabrey had yet to become reality.

She shouted his name and his face turned almost blindly in her direction, lit by the displays in the neck-ring of his suit.

"You go," she told Remus and the others. "You get out."

"If he is a god, he doesn't need your help," Hailfoot said. But it wasn't quite that. Gods didn't need human help, by definition. As far as her experience with Rabbit went, gods didn't help humans much either. That indistinct divinity had evaporated the moment its people had needed it. Guy had led them to victory against the plant god, and she knew he would have a plan for the other two monstrous deities that had descended to claim the world. But he had used the Seagull and he had used her, to make his plan a reality. And when he had gone to build his promised land in the night sky, he had taken all those other people she'd seen in Beaker's image. Guy was the god of using people, which meant he was the god who needed people's help.

She vaulted the first gap between broken roofs without much difficulty. Smoke blew past her face, and then it was insects, a straggle of them getting caught in her hair and scrabbling at her face. The shocking lances of pain as they stung whatever they touched, as their outsized mandibles hooked into her skin. She tore them off, slapped at them, kept moving. Another jump, and then she'd be within a final vault of Guy and all the anti-ant measures he could surely deploy.

Her footing gave. She'd love to blame the ants undermining it, but likely it was just old concrete, cracked by rain and sun and the thread-like roots of weeds. Three storeys up and her forward leap had suddenly pivoted to a plunge. Below her was a seething darkness, insects on tarmac and no hard divisions between the two.

A hand caught her, two fingers hooking into the cord she used as a belt. She felt it stretch, strain. Her flailing hand found a strong wrist. *Guy*. Except he was still ahead of her and his powers hadn't yet extended to being in two places at once.

Sinewy strength hauled her back to safety and she practically bounced off the broad chest of Beaker. His eyeglasses caught the firelight like autumn moons. A moment of mouth open, questions thronging, save that he had surely been following the same path she was. He had been seeking the protections of Guy the god. Or else he had been after her, to be sure that she and the god did not just abandon the Seagull to their fate.

A frozen moment, trying to work out if he was about to knife her or throw her from the building. Whether she should be trying to do the same with him. Then something gave beneath them, a low groan of strained structure. These buildings were all ruins anyway, and the fire or the gnawing of the insects had cracked something load-bearing.

The world slid sideways. Beaker's grip on her arm clenched like a vice, momentarily so painful that ants and falling and burning all became background worries in comparison. Yet she clung right back because he seemed the one fixed point in the whole world right then.

They came down in a great sloughing of broken concrete, the solid walls of the building fracturing into scales still drunkenly strung together on corded metal bones. Instantly there were ants seething up from every crack, heedless of how many of their siblings had been crushed. Beaker cast something down and it spread a flower of flame about them, enough that Amri had to beat out the embers alighting in her clothes and on her legs. In its light, Beaker found the least ant-busy road and ran for it. He dragged her three steps in his wake and then let go, leaving it to her if she wanted to follow.

She did, because it was that or the ants cleaning her bones of the least fragments of flesh.

Beaker ran between the sudden gout of the flames he was casting down, that licked at his heels even as the insects crackled and exploded in them. There were drifts of them everywhere, Amri realised. Insects crushed, burned, choked by the smoke or just dead in that way insects died. That specific insect mortality of vast numbers gone without any tear shed, because there were always more, and the gods, who might mark the fall of sparrows, lacked the fine resolution to care for insects. The insect god least of all, who sent these myriad legions to their doom. The one care he would have of them would be to send more ants to recover the tiny curled corpses, food for the next generation to come boiling out of the earth.

Beaker had stopped. The hatched clay globe he was weighing in his hands was his last, she understood.

It wasn't an insuperable wall of ants that had halted him. There was a figure ahead, as glaringly out of place as all these new ideas seething about the inside of Amri's head.

Guy, she thought, but it wasn't. A humanoid figure, slightly crooked as though some connections across its hips and shoulders were offset. The flames cast light on smooth features that were familiar from the broken thing the plant god had crushed in his vines. Its body was articulated, artificial, blandly male.

"Guy's little friends," said the same voice that broken thing had used, now issuing from this undamaged mouth.

"You're the other one," Beaker said. "The plastic god."

"I am his ambassador, save that nobody cares about diplomacy anymore." The thing's mouth moved, but not quite with the words. When it stepped forwards there was a queasy smoothness to its movements, nothing of either suddenness or hesitancy, the poles between which living movement was strung. "Come with me."

"Or what?" Beaker demanded.

"Or be devoured." The plastic man turned and walked deliberately away. Amri saw that the insects around its feet were dead, as though some invisible poison was seeping between its joints. She hurried to catch up with it, and Beaker followed, stamping on the advancing fringe of the ant army as it rushed to take up the slack.

"I am the good god." And the smooth head turned entirely backwards to speak to them, even as the automaton strode on. "I do not seek to tear down or consume. I only wish to preserve what we have of the world. To recreate the wonders that once were. I can preserve you, also. Come with me"—and a weird sound that Amri realised was meant to be laughing—"if you want to live."

14.

PANTHEON

"I HAD HOPED to bring Guy," Padreig Gramm said. "I hope he'll come anyway."

"To get us, you mean?" Beaker growled. "Don't think he's sentimental that way."

Padreig spread perfectly white, almost unlined hands. "Or just for old time's sake. We go way back, he and I."

The journey out of the Seagull camp and across the river hadn't been easy. The ants had swarmed all about them, but the seething host had been fixated on the plastic ambassador rather than the two humans. Or on the succession of ambassadors. Each had left a swathe of insect corpses in its wake, a crunching road of minute death that Guy could certainly follow if he had a mind to. Each had, one by one, been overcome, the little bodies fouling their joints, mandibles chewing their way inside through the thin, stretchy stuff that didn't look quite like skin, through eyes and ears and mouths. A succession of mannequins had stumbled to a frozen halt just as the next arrived to guide them on, left on the road like grotesque signposts.

And now they were here, in Gramm's personal wonderland, and it was... wondrous, in a way.

Instead of just tearing down buildings, or raising a dirt spire fit for a deity, Padreig was restoring the city. Or that was how it had seemed. They'd arrived and found gleaming square towers again, red brick and brown stone frontages. Hedonistic spans of uncracked glass displaying a baffling array of objects and writing that Beaker squinted at, lips moving. Most of it was utterly outside Amri's frame of reference, but some of the things seemed to be food, and some of them clothes, displayed on lesser, static plastic people, some lacking heads or human contours entirely. A few displays had glittering tablets like the cracked relic Beaker possessed, each showing a different magical moving image.

"You've seen what the others want to do," Padreig told them, when they'd been led into his presence. "Horrible things. We argued. It was a shame. We all wanted to reinvigorate this dead world, you see, but... I mean, why? Aggressive rewilding and... insects. Nothing but insects."

"It is," the shivering voice of Matthias Fabrey insisted, "the efficient path. A route to automation of tasks that remains entirely organic and sustainable."

Amri hadn't liked that he was present too. Or, not present but with a kind of representative that made her shudder to see it. Honestly, though, she hadn't liked much of anything she'd seen.

The ambassador—the final one that had got the two of them into Padreig's dominion—had led them into one of the buildings. She'd braced herself for a great labyrinth of restored rooms, glowing images on every wall, grasping for an idea of *what it was like* and picturing only a better version of the Rabbit village where there were extra people around to do the menial tasks.

Instead, inside it was a shell. Just a great cage of silvery scaffolding soaring up, covered over with some thin covering that didn't even keep out the wind much. What she saw outside had been an illusion, just as Guy had rolled out for the Seagull.

"A work in progress," Gramm explained. He was sitting at one end of a long table—a thing of polished black plastic with metal legs. There were chairs of the same style and she and Beaker sat down warily, keeping their distance. He had a couple of dogs flanking him. Or at least, they were metal and headless, but something in their pose communicated the canine.

Padreig Gramm was very much the man from the image she'd seen. Young, smooth, weirdly dead-looking. A lack of animation in his face, and nothing at all that reached his eyes. More alive than his plastic people, but only just.

She could still hear the murmured conversations of the plastic people outside. Talk was most of what they did, or showing one another pictures. They'd seemed very engaged in it. Some had even come to blows. She'd tried to listen in and heard a weird melange of language, words she knew, but no context. Weirdly mundane talk of cats and meals and weather, references to stories and myths she didn't know, obscenities, arguments using incomprehensible insults, over insignificant things. On and on, and all of it at once.

"I object to being characterised as 'the insect god,'" Fabrey whispered. "It is merely a path to rebuilding the world. Biological robots superior to their artificial counterparts. They multiply. They adapt and solve problems with a very simple toolkit. Little building blocks that will allow me to create a new world."

"I can't allow you," Padreig told him. "Whatever world you'd end up with would still be all over bugs and that's displeasing. I wish you'd just stop it and come over in person. I can save you. I am going to preserve everyone and everything for the future."

Fabrey made a derisive noise. His avatar was a board hung up on one wall like a picture. A thousand tiny moth-like things had been glued to it. As they frantically struggled to get free, the sequential rustle of their wings produced his voice.

Beaker's relic had emitted a soft chime when they'd come in, and now he had it in his lap, below the level of the table. Amri glanced over and saw the little screen alight with images and characters. As the two gods bickered he leant sideways and murmured, "It has found connection."

"What's that?"

"The library and marketplace of things that once was. It's here. The mirror has found the door to it. Look." He showed her a little sequence of moving moments. Guy and Padreig shaking hands, radiating hearty goodwill. Bespectacled

Matthias with some of the other people they'd seen before. A fiery spear ascending into the heavens. Something like scaffolding hanging in the night sky as the invisible eye of the viewer moved past it, seeing tiny motes that were people in suits like Guy's, which coasted about, bringing panels and struts to add to the skeletal construction. A great green world of flourishing trees and plants, except the horizon curved the wrong way and a bright logo splashed across the screen to obscure the details.

"Is Bruce really dead, though?" Padreig asked, breaking into her reverie.

Amri glanced guiltily up and nodded hurriedly.

"Such a loss," the man said. "I would have saved him."

"Why?" Beaker demanded. "He was a monster."

"Not his powers, but him. The man he was and had been," the plastic god explained. "He was one of us. The great visionaries and innovators, the pinnacle of this world, back when it was living. And I can reconstruct him, like I have the people outside, but it's not quite the same. I know you've gained access to some of my archives with your device. You'll see there what he once was. A great man. A genius. A rare mind, as we all were. Ah! And speaking of such..."

By that point—sitting at the table listening to one god eulogise another while the mouthpiece of a third whirred and battered at its prison on the wall—Amri thought she had reached some hard threshold of strangeness. Then one of the plastic people entered, carrying on the palm of its outstretched hand a tray, upon which sat a head. It was a head like those of the artificial people, but with more definition and ornament, the lips painted gold, the eyes like shards of coloured glass. It was set before Padreig and its bearer retreated with a bow.

"You're there, then?" Padreig asked. "Guy?"

The head's mouth moved, echoing the words issuing from it. "You could have just built a phone. Using entire severed heads speaks of madness." The voice was Guy's.

"One uses what one has lying around," Padreig said. "I was just lamenting Bruce."

"Don't."

The god of plastics sighed. "Well, we're all here, then. I'm well aware, Matti, that you're currently launching some sort of assault against me, and I'm deploying quite the cocktail of insecticides, so you may as well stop it."

"We evolve and adapt," the insect god murmured.

"At least save your doomed armies until you've heard my offer."

"They're just bugs," Fabrey said. "I can make more. *They* can make more. It's what bugs do."

"Pat," came Guy's voice from the head.

"Yes, I know, you've crept in somewhere under cover of the civil disturbance. Pray my avatars find you before you get eaten by ants." Gramm shook his head ruefully. "This isn't how I wanted any of this to go, my friends. I sincerely hope it isn't how you wanted it either. And Bruce is *dead*."

"Good riddance," rustled the wings. Fabrey's voice was fading as more and more of the glued moths expired.

"Listen," Gramm told the insects and the head. "I want

to save you. Your insights, your minds. I'll recreate you anyway, just like I'm doing with everyone else, but if you come to me then I can do more. Greater fidelity for posterity."

"Excuse me," Amri said.

Gramm visibly recalled that she existed.

"What are you doing?" she asked.

When he just blinked at her, Beaker put in, "With your talking plastic puppets. What's that about?"

"Tell them," Guy's voice prompted. "They're brighter than you'd think."

"I'm recreating the world," Padreig said simply, as though to a child. "Our world. The old Earth, but before things went bad. No wild jungle, no global anthill, just the world, the way it was. Our global world where to think of something was to have it made halfway around the planet and then put into your hand for free. Because what made our world was the people. Millions of people in a great marketplace of ideas, exchanging the currency of their brains effortlessly, and every word recorded and preserved. I kept it all. It's the world, my friends. The world as people saw it and said it, and now I am recreating it and everyone in it."

"You've made a collection of shoddy robots and you've programmed them to read out social media?" Guy summarised. "I honestly just thought I hadn't understood what you were after, but that's actually it?"

"Ants don't sound so bad now, do they?" Fabrey whispered.

"They are not robots," Padreig said with dignity. "They are Self-Driving People. I have invented them. They are not programmed. They are governed by an algorithm that recreates genuine human interactions based on those they had back in the old days. They are humanity, restored."

"That's... not humanity," Guy objected. "It's just a lot of talking heads in an echo chamber."

"What's the difference?" Padreig asked blankly. "Come and talk, Guy."

"So you can make a plastic man with my face?"

"Yes," Padreig said—Amri felt it should have been a heartfelt exaltation, but the man wasn't built for them. "Look, Guy, we all dealt with time in our own way. I don't want to imagine what kind of wizened ant-fed thing is in that big tower Matti's built, and Bruce wasn't much more than a mushroom by the end. You've had your body re-engineered, I know, and probably you've got a few centuries left before your patented replacement organs start to go, but then what? Let me preserve you for the future, please." A twitch animated part of his face briefly. "Ah, one of my sentries just caught a glimpse of you. Just ahead of the ants. I imagine you're after these two. That's why I brought them here. You've doubtless triangulated the location of this terminal by now. Come on in. Come be part of my grand experiment. And Matti, the door's still open."

"I will take your door," came the last failing dregs of the moths, "and fill it with ants."

A hard plastic hand landed on Amri's shoulder. An escort had arrived, moving with alarming quiet. A quartet of plastic people. One had ragged, pocked skin where the ants had been at it.

"I'm moving your friends to a place of safety, for leverage purposes," Padreig told the head. "Assuming they're of any value. Come on in, Guy, I'll be waiting. Together we'll see off this pest problem and then set to remaking the future, eh?"

If Guy had a witticism in response, Amri didn't hear it as she was hustled from the room.

15.

REAR-VIEW MIRROR

THEY WERE IN a bunker. A cavernous space which must have served some function for a grand building long collapsed and cleared away. As everything had been cleared, Amri realised. Padreig talked about restoring a past, but to do so he had to wipe the cluttered slate clean first. She wondered if the Self-Driving People did it, or whether he had larger machines.

"Guy will find us?" She'd not meant it as a question, but it came out that way.

Beaker grunted. He was sitting on a heap of stone that had been shoved down here. His device was in his hands and he moved it around irritably. "Trying to reconnect," he said shortly, when she asked him.

Up top, things had smelled weird, a kind of sting in the nose that spoke of nothing living. Or, when the wind changed, it smelled of the acid reek of fighting ants. The armies of Matthias Fabrey were still pressing the attack.

Amri could only hope they didn't get this far, because she'd be a rat in a trap if they did.

The smell down here was of decay. Because there was little else to do but annoy Beaker, she went exploring to the edge of the light that came down from above. More rubble, the piecemeal corpses of the buildings Padreig had levelled so he could put up his facades.

Bodies.

They were all mixed in with the fractured concrete, and the light was poor. It took her too long to understand that some of the things projecting from the cracks had fingers. But of course someone had lived here before Padreig came, just as the Rabbit had lived where the plant god claimed. She tried to remember who they might have been. Mad Dog, perhaps, or Foxcat. Dead now, anyway. She hoped some had survived to flee.

She retreated back to Beaker, hunched over the little lit-up relic that had reopened the door to the great library of images and words he'd found before. The sight of the big, scarred man hunched over the little thing with the absorption of a child was weirdly incongruous.

"You were always a monster." She hadn't meant to say it, but right now so many things had happened that she felt detached from the world and her own body. Thoughts issued from her mouth with the automatic bustle of the ants.

Beaker glanced up and plainly understood what she meant. "When I was a sprat," he said, "I had a friend. Beach Dog caught us in their territory. Chased us. Nowhere to run but the mud. Tide caught him and he died. Me too, almost. Helpless, we were. That's what I took away from that. Mud and water and their spears, and us with no leverage against the world to push back. And when that happens, the world kills you as it wants. Since then, I've been all about the levers. How to make the world do what I want, and stop it doing what *it* wants, to me and mine. That means you got to be strong to shove back, but it's more than that. It's up here, too." Tapping at his head. "Got to understand. Understand the world that came before because we're still living in it. Even though it's dead and broken too."

"The gods must scare the crap out of you," she said, those ant-words just marching out still.

She saw where he might have taken offence, but instead he just nodded. No friend of hers really, but another rat in the same trap. "So look for a lever. Here are the gods." Showing her the little screen. At first, that group of strangers with the four gods in their midst, but then he was showing her other things he'd found, hunting through that invisible library. Enthusiastic voices talking in that strange, half-comprehensible way about great futures. Life in space, salvation for humanity, Utopia. Guy himself, that slighter, younger Guy, smiling at them with brilliant, perfect teeth.

"This is the future we're building," he said, eyes flashing with the inspiration of it all. "Cities in space. Green cities, wild spaces, transplanted species. Imagine your commute…" The view changed to show images that were almost but not completely real: people entering a windowed capsule suspended from a rail; travelling through a bizarre upcurving landscape. Then the viewpoint pulling back, through the wall, so that the whole was revealed as a ring floating in the night, and then many rings. A sky-crowding conurbation of revolving parts like a hypnagogic vision of interlocking wheels and eyes so that Amri couldn't look at it.

"It's all out there waiting for us," said Guy, as though to dream it was to bring it full-formed into being. And perhaps for him it was.

The next video was so real she couldn't tell if it was actually the record of things that had been, or if it was more fakery. There were people in strange one-piece garments jogging down a path, trees on either side, that same inverted horizon. Elsewhere, higher in the sky, people flew with gossamer wings. There were buildings that went all the way up, stretching vertiginously until they became the base of a different building that had its foundations in the sky. They were lit up like suns in many colours, and people jogged in and out of them. Machines with wheels and arms were at work where panels had been removed. *Building anew*, she thought at first, but then, *Repairing?*

Beaker passed his hands across the screen, moving from one scene of unspeakable beauty to another. Laughing people played strange sports, walked with arms about each other. People in suits floated against the dark of the sky. Machines coasted silently in the void, carrying people to places she couldn't even imagine. Great rocks, cracked into pieces and harvested for metals. Tangles of scaffolding that would become more utopias for more people removed from overhot, underfed Earth.

And she understood that some of it might be real, and some of it might just be illusions created to show people what was *going* to be real, and over it all were the forceful, enthusiastic voices telling her how wonderful it all was. But it *was* wonderful. Like a dream, or a story. She felt tears come to her eyes, seeing all those healthy, beautiful people going about their lives in idle bliss. Not one of them sick or starving or crippled. Perfect.

Beaker grunted, and she saw from his face it wasn't what he was after. Not *leverage*, nor even understanding. Nothing he could ever replicate or use against the gods. And whatever the gods were going to build here on Earth now they'd returned, she knew that it wouldn't have space for her. However friendly Padreig had appeared, the bodies amongst the rubble showed that. And Fabrey would just cut her into a million shreds to feed to his hungry children.

Guy, then.

Except maybe he was dead already, or maybe he had fled, or come to some deal with Padreig. Or didn't care.

She watched him talking again. He was in space now, or at least wearing a suit that was a simpler shadow of his current one. He was explaining something, showing children playing a game of impossible leaps and gradual falls. In the background, more machines worked, and she saw with a shock that the green vista had been an illusion, because they'd taken a whole panel of it out, leaving a dark mess of burnt-looking metal roots behind. Guy didn't seem to mind, though. He was gesturing at everything but that, smiling like the sun.

Beaker snarled and smudged his thumb across the screen again. Everything froze for a moment and he swore, but then he had a long branching tree of little icons with words in a script so tiny he had to move his lenses in and out before he found some meaning in them.

The voice they heard, in that final sequence, was Guy's. She wasn't sure if the distant figure was his, but who else could it be? A single figure walking through that verdant wonderland, the landscape that only rose away on all sides until it met itself overhead, coming the other way. The fields, the trees, the little perfect clusters of homes. And one figure, in a heavy, helmeted suit, trudging through it from a great distance.

"We were always going back." Guy, fiercely emphatic so that she can imagine his *go-with-me* smile. "We were never going to abandon Earth. We have a duty. That's why we're going. A positive duty to the old place, to bring it back to life. That's why. Now we've conquered space. Built Utopia." And that one trudging traveller, heavily suited against the vacant perfection all around it.

"It's what we came out here for," a new voice came tinnily from the device. Bruce Mayall, who would become the plant god. "A blank slate, mate. Room to build."

"Well, a certain amount of biomass." That must be Fabrey. And she understood this wasn't the keen speaking-to-camera upselling of the other images. This was something more candid, recorded presumably by Gramm, the one not speaking.

"Easily removed," Guy's voice replied.

"Or used. If you'll just look at my—"

"We'll have plenty of time to argue that over on the way there," Bruce put in. "Seriously, Matti, it's not going to be bugs. For now, though—"

"I'm coming," Guy confirmed.

"Sentimental," Fabrey accused.

"Not at all. But it felt wrong not to take one last look."

"I'm recording it. I'm recording all of it." Padreig Gramm at last, sounding closer, but also hushed, and she understood he was speaking so the others couldn't hear.

The suited figure was tiny now, and the light of the world was closing in on them. A darkness fell on everything she could see, square by square at random. And where the light wasn't, the trees and houses weren't either. There was just the darkness, and scarred infrastructure, ducts and cables and holes through which the dark of a sunless sky clawed through. Drifting motes of ruin that might have been anything.

"We'll bring life back to the old world," Guy's voice went on, sounding exactly like all those earlier voices then, the ones telling you how wonderful it all was. "Now we're done here."

The recording ended, and Beaker didn't move onto another. He just turned the device off and sat there, staring into the dark where the corpses were. Amri opened her mouth a couple of times, but wasn't quite sure what to say. She didn't think she'd understood it. The words and the images hadn't matched, and that made her wonder about all the other words and images.

Then there was a rattle of stones above, and they both leapt up. It wasn't more plastic people, though. Cutting into the square of sunlight, casting down a line of rubbery cabling, was Guy.

16.

POISON

"You ever sowed seed?" Guy asked them. Out of the rubble pit, away from the slow putrefaction it hid, he had them perched on a spur of rubble within one of the big frame buildings.

Amri nodded. Beaker shook his head.

"Going to need you to get good at it. When we leave here, you start spreading this around." He had little paper bags of white powder for them. "It's something Bruce designed, because he knew that if Matti got his mandibles dug in, then the Empire of the Plants was going to have problems. Bugs and plants have been running an arms race for millions of years. This was Bruce's ultimate weapon. Only all his facilities were vegetable-based and I couldn't use them, so I had to come here and borrow Pat's chemical printers on the sly."

"And now?" Beaker asked.

"Spread it around. It's all over ants, out there, but they

should go for this in preference to you."

"Should?" Amri echoed.

"Mostly should," Guy agreed.

"And what is it?"

"Ant food. To solve our little pest problem. You know how to poison ants, right? No point just leaving out something that'll kill the individuals. You want something that tastes super-yummy so they bring it back to the nest."

"And then they all die?"

Guy smiled bleakly. "Well, in this case it's not quite that simple. It's not poison, per se. Bruce really did have a good idea before he died. I'm glad to honour his memory by putting it into practice. But first, we need some good take-up and early adoption by our insect brethren. So let's get going."

Thus armed, he led them out again, ducking under the filmy sheet that the 'building' was made from, momentarily making the entire edifice ripple and quake as though seen through water. Guy glanced up at it.

"Mad, really," he said. "He's building a virtual layer to all this. Here." He snatched Beaker's relic, swiped away everything that was shown there and then held it up. The screen had become a magic lens onto whatever it was pointed at. Through that enchanted eye, the plastic people had real faces, wore strange, bright clothes. The buildings had depth and detail lacking in their projected fronts. "What you see for real, it's all just placeholder stuff," Guy said. "This is the heart of it."

Then they turned a corner and it was a battlefield. Of sorts.

The Self-Driving People were striding about, exuding a clear liquid that left mounds of curled-up ant corpses in their wake as whatever toxins it contained got to work. Plenty of them were halted or on the ground, though, vital parts of their structure severed or melted by the endless waves of tiny aggressors.

"Off you go," Guy said.

"What about you?" Beaker demanded.

"You've got the stuff now. Clear a way and I'll follow."

They did so, and whatever chemical the plastic people were using to attract the ants couldn't compete with the white powder. The insects went mad for it, forming rolling balls fighting to gather it up. Soon there were trains of little porters proudly bearing the confection back in the direction of Matti's tower.

"This place is about to become hella busy," Guy said. "Those are going to tell the rest that it's gourmet ant luncheon in this neighbourhood." As always, the words that were alien and impenetrable, and the sense that came through.

When the bags were empty, Guy declared it was time to make themselves scarce, but first he needed to check one thing. "Want to make sure that Pat's still engaged."

He took them inwards, past the war zone to where the Self-Driving People still stood and talked vacantly. Amri looked at them through the eye of Beaker's device, seeing nearly human faces flick between lifelike expressions. Individuals, strangers, men, women, children. Laughter, anger, despair, warmth. A lost world of humanity that died when the gods left.

"The world," she said, handing the thing back to Beaker. "You left it."

"To build something better," Guy agreed.

"Utopia."

"The dream," he agreed. "Earth was dying. It was full of people wasting their lives. And we'd made the best of it. We'd tried to enrich those lives, expand their minds, give people what they wanted. We'd provided them with more ways to talk to each other, more ways to fulfil their every need than humans had ever had before. Were they grateful? Did they get onboard with our grand project? They did not. And Earth was dying. Everyone could see. So we took the smart people who understood us, and we went to build somewhere better. We took the brains and the resources and the ideas, so they wouldn't just be wasted. Like water into dry sand, right? You understand that."

Amri was thinking of the images Beaker had found, and didn't know *what* she understood, but she nodded.

"You can't imagine how frustrating it was," Guy said, and that was probably true. "To have a head full of these genius ideas, and everyone on Earth trying to shackle you. Governments and shareholders and just regular people bitching about it, trying to tie your hands, to take your stuff, to *complain*, when what would they have without us? We four, the greatest minds of the greatest age of humanity."

"Couldn't you stop the end of that world?" The words were out before Amri could stop them. She braced for divine displeasure, but Guy just shrugged.

"They wouldn't have let us," he told her. "They were always telling us what we should do, with what we'd made. Always thought they had a right to what we'd created. They wouldn't have let us do it our way." There was more, but by then they could hear the voices from the non-building ahead. Padreig, in conversation with Guy.

They even peeked in. There was the table, there the head on its platter. The god of plastics leant forwards, gesticulating, obviously keen to score some conversational point.

"Billions," he said, "eventually. Of course it's only millions now. So many people we have only minimal record of, not enough to reconstruct. But everyone who was *engaged* with society before, on any meaningful level, has left themselves recorded in the datasphere."

"They've left what they wrote online," the head said with Guy's voice.

"The algorithm can reconstruct them from that. As much as is necessary," Padreig insisted. "Real people, reconstructed from their own thoughts. And once I've finished my little debugging-with-extreme-prejudice, I can begin exponential growth. I've already solved the resource issue. Anything and everything carbon-based can be reconstructed as plastics." A mirthless grin. "You remember when plastics were part of the problem, with fossil fuels and all that? Now they're part of the solution. All that atmospheric carbon sequestered in plastics. The oxygen too. To build seven billion Self-Driving People and all the servers required to run them."

"That sounds like a lot of energy. That sounds like a lot of heat."

"Then we build a lot of fans. And outside my cities, it won't matter how hot it gets. There won't be anything to mind. No downsides, Guy. It's all ready for us. I know Bruce is dead, and Matti is proving intractable, but you and me... We were always the *really* smart ones, right? We were the ones who saw how it was going to go. Just come in, with your real body. I'm sure that before conditions have become intolerable for life, we'll have solved the upload problem."

"You're sure?" Guy's voice queried.

Amri looked from the man beside her to the head on the table. "Have you been talking to him all the time you were with us?"

"Pat thinks I have." Guy shrugged. "It's a chatbot. Basically the same sort of thing as Pat's poor plastic people are running. Just an algorithm that can endlessly turn out things that sound like the sort of things I might say, in the context of getting Pat to keep talking. You'd think he'd have noticed. But he always did like talking about himself."

GUY'S DRONES FOUND the survivors of the Seagull and the Rabbit eventually. They'd done exactly the opposite of what Amri had thought. They'd moved into Cockroach territory and ended up as guests of the locals. Not, as Guy said, a euphemism; genuine guests.

There were still plenty of ants busily coursing in long glittering roads that radiated out from the grand spire. Amri could see other spires too, amongst the ruins of the city. A network of lines across the world, made by and of insects.

None of it seemed to be slowing down, and though there were plenty of dead ants, they didn't seem to be dying in their thousands as she'd expected.

"It failed," Beaker summarised. "Your poison."

"It wasn't poison," Guy said. "You notice we're not being swarmed, right?"

"You have something that keeps them away," Amri suggested.

"A sound. A smell," the Seagull agreed.

"I mean, I have, but I haven't deployed it yet. And I'd have to keep changing it up because the little bastards are tenacious and keep finding their way round the edges of things. But right now these are just ants doing ant things."

Amri had been braced for ant things. Specifically ants picking the bones of the entire Cockroach people. Or else the Seagull and her own handful of kin staked out as sacrifices for Matthias Fabrey. Instead of which they reached the odd trash-pile huts of the Cockroach, in the very shadow of the ant god's spire, and somehow everyone was still alive.

"They were fixing to give us up," Hailfoot told her. "The Roach. They had some kind of weird deal going on with the god. But then the ants... changed. Suddenly they were just ants."

By that time, Guy had gone up to the actual slopes of the spire. He was using some defence so that the ants parted around him, because Amri reckoned even ants doing ant things would have been hungrily investigating him otherwise, but it was the only prominent pulpit he could use to speak down to everyone. And the Cockroach people gathered for his words amiably enough. They weren't farmers like the Rabbit—save for mushrooms—nor hunters like the Seagull. Just scavengers with low expectations in life. Not being devoured by ants had been quite enough for them. And now, Amri saw, that shoe was on the other tiny foot. As they gathered to hear what Guy had to say, plenty of them had sticks covered in ants, stuck there by some sort of fungal paste but still alive. The Roach people licked the wriggling bugs from their skewers, chewed placidly, and listened.

"Your god is dead," Guy proclaimed. "I'm the replacement."

The Roach shrugged along with that, popped mushrooms and ate ants. It seemed all much of a muchness to them. Guy looked a little put out that declaring deicide hadn't brought out some furious priestly caste to excommunicate him. The Roach were sanguine, though. One god was as good as another, and if Guy abandoned them, then no god would be fine too. Failboy, their tripping priest, was more than happy to put a garland of silvery trash round Guy's neck and let him get on with things, which he plainly found galling.

"You'd think it would mean something. The death of their insect god," he said to Beaker and Amri later. They'd found him sitting alone, overlooking the Roach as they harvested ants with a minimum of effort. Their lack of excitement had knocked him back more than Amri would have thought.

The Seagull shrugged. "Roaches are worthless. We didn't even raid them much. They never had anything to take. So how did you kill him, then?" A sharp look. "He was in there, to kill?"

"Of course."

"Only your plastic god said 'upload,' and that means putting your mind in another thing."

Guy blinked at Beaker's understanding of the term. Amri had been thinking in the same way, though. Because when the gods left for space, that had been hundreds of years ago. Nobody lived that long, and yet here they were.

"We are still those people," Guy explained. "The science of our day—*our* science, that we pioneered out in Utopia—has let us replace and preserve. I'm stronger and fitter now than I ever was. And yet… there's a limit. So, yes, we were looking into uploads, Pat most of all. Our minds running on the greatest computers ever created, forever, unfettered by the limits of the human brain. That's the dream."

"But it didn't happen," Beaker said. "The plant god had a body. You have one. The plastic god does, we saw."

"Something happened," Guy said. His odd melancholy seemed to open him up, put him off his guard. He wasn't fencing like he usually did. "We got something, in the computer. Something that talked like us. More than those sad puppets that Pat's convinced are people. Something that could even insist it was us, give orders. Beg."

"Beg?" Amri asked.

"We shut it down," Guy said flatly. "It didn't *feel* like us. This us, these bodies, *they* were us, even though they were so heavily modified. Even though they grow old despite everything. And the voice in the computer was just… a voice. And by then we'd built algorithms so sophisticated, how could we ever tell if it was really us in there, or just some engine throwing together words that seemed to make sense because we'd programmed it too well? We shut them all down. Only Pat was left trying to make it work, in the end. Probably he'll kid himself that he has, eventually. For the rest of us, it was physical bodies for as long as we could. Long enough for us to come back here and build something.

"So yes, Matti was in there, at the heart of the colony. His actual, original self, whatever was left of it. And now he's dead. I killed him, like I did Bruce. Because we all knew that there'd only be one left in the end."

"His ants fed him your poison," Beaker guessed.

"Not even that." Guy seemed curiously deflated. "Bruce's concoction just… denatured the pheromones he was using to tell the ants what to do. They cut him off from his crawling congregation. Turned him from an *us* to a *them*."

"And then what?" Amri pressed.

Guy shrugged. "They ate him, I imagine. Alive. Piece by piece."

In the silence that occasioned, Amri noted a scarecrow figure slouching sidelong over towards them, cloaked in rags. Iffy the Roach.

"We found one of the plastic men," he told Guy when he arrived. "It had an announcement. The other god is declaring that he's the winner."

"Probably." Guy took a deep breath and then pushed himself to his feet. "I need to go look inside an anthill. Because Matti was working towards something before I did for him, and hopefully it's something I can use."

17.

SUMMIT OF OLYMPUS

By the time Guy came back out of the insect god's spire, there was quite a crowd awaiting him. Word of the god-killer had spread.

"Who've we got here?" he asked Amri and Beaker. He didn't seem surprised at the new additions.

"Halfbeak Pigeons," Amri said. "Clawfoot, some of them." Said with bitterness, because they'd turned their backs on her people before, but now two gods were dead they'd deigned to send some spears.

"Mad Dogs, a few who got out from under the plastics god," Beaker added. "Mongrel Dogs. Pit Bulls. Basically a lot of dogs. A few Foxcats. Rats, some of them, come slinking back. We'd have cut their throats, only…" An awkward, averted glance. "Didn't think you'd want it. Oh, and more Roaches than anyone ever knew there were. Way too many Roaches, all sitting round eating ants 'n' shrooms like it's a holiday."

"And Pat?"

"We sent some scouts over there," Beaker confirmed. "The one who got furthest in dropped dead. Plastic people didn't touch him, he just... grabbed at his throat and died. There are more of the puppets than there were. There's a big machine that's making them. Making killing air too, we think."

"Sounds about right," Guy agreed. "The killing air will just be a side effect, honestly. Pat's not going to send robots out to kill you by hand. He'll just do his thing until the act of it has made the world so inhospitable even the ants can't survive it."

"You have a way to kill him now? The bug god had it?"

Guy smiled. "It can be done. And I want to tell him that. I want to see his reaction."

Amri remembered the face of the plastic god, and didn't think it was made for reactions, much. "He sends plastic people to us, asking for you. He still wants you to come and join him."

"He's not getting one of those marionettes with my words in its mouth," Guy decided briskly. "But I'll speak to the next mouthpiece he sends over. It's time to settle this war in heaven once and for all."

"Well, good," Beaker said forcefully. "The Seagull's ready, all of us on our feet from the last fight. Got forty, maybe fifty Dog soldiers, got Foxcats, Clawfoots and Halfbeaks, maybe a dozen. And the same of Roaches who'll actually fight, though they say they're doing it for their dead bug god. The rest won't pick up a sharp stick in anger, but they're keeping us fed." His face twisted to show what he thought of the fare. "We got prybars, picks, hooks. We got sledges and mauls. I've seen those plastic boys, and we can pull them apart easy enough." He yanked at the bandana about his neck. "We soak these in piss and ant-water, keeps out the poison as much as we can. We bring the fire like we did against the plants. Then you do your god-thing when we've made a wedge for you."

Guy was smiling slightly. "You have it all worked out," he remarked mildly.

"My aunt did not survive the insect god," Beaker said flatly, and Amri realised with a shock that, no, she hadn't seen the old woman who led the Seagull since their return to the camp.

Beaker's face was hard and flushed with anger. "It is time for the god war to end."

"On that we agree," Guy said smoothly. "But all this sabre-rattling won't be necessary. There's a better way forward than just throwing lives away. Because, if it comes to it, you can be sure Pat has some nasty last-ditch surprises." He smiled past Beaker. "I think the time has come for negotiation instead. Amri, tell me what 'negotiation' means, will you?"

She blinked. "Middle ground. When there is an argument. I give, you give, we agree."

"I suspect Pat probably thinks the same," Guy said sweetly. "Let me tell both of you, 'negotiation' just means getting what you want in a way that means the other person gives it up of their own free will. I've got the measure of Pat.

You've heard him. He's all *preserve this, record that,* even if it means destroying everything he isn't interested in. He wants me as his faithful apprentice. He's soft plastic. That's what I see when I look at him. Lacks the courage of his convictions. Needs someone else to tell him how good his ideas are. You know what he sees when he looks at me?"

Amri and Beaker exchanged a look.

"He sees a man who's already killed two gods," Guy told them flatly. "And you can be sure that'll be uppermost in his mind when he comes to the table to talk."

They didn't have a proper table, like Gramm had. Instead, around twenty of the Cockroach brought a big slab of concrete and set it on four smaller chunks, then spent far too long obsessively filing bits down in situ until the whole was relatively level. Iffy and Failboy presented the whole to Guy as though it was the most ancient of sacred sites, fit for a god.

"When this is done," he told Amri, "a temple here, I think."

"A... temple?"

"Big house, purpose-built for a god to live in," he said impatiently. "Maybe a statue of me on the outside. Look, if I'm going to be living among you folks as your great saviour, then I'm going to need some pomp, right? Something to impress the neighbours, so they come pay tribute and agree that your tribe's the best. A temple for the god who saved the world, I don't think that's asking too much. This is just shabby."

But when Beaker and the others had assembled the warband behind him, all spears and salvage-metal swords and glass-studded clubs—when he had stepped forwards in the armour of his suit, with his drones roosting on his shoulders—there was something that spoke to Amri there. Something of gods and myths and a lost world of magic. Even Failboy's jabbering died down to a mutter.

Amri stepped forward, twisting aside from Beaker's attempt to hook her back, and went to stand beside Guy. Because, if he was talking about temples and worship, then he'd need a high priestess, and right now she had no other prospects in the world. This was her one slender chance to catch destiny by the tail as it rushed past.

The ambassador sent by Padreig Gramm wore an attempt at the man's own face. Given the original's lack of animation, Amri wouldn't have thought that was much of a task, but somehow it had gone wrong anyway, a crooked mould-line disfiguring it like a scar. The eyes were blank hemispheres almost as expressionless as the originals. A watchful lens nestled in the cables of the puppet's open throat.

"I'm glad you've decided to be reasonable, Guy." Gramm's voice issued from the thing's chest, the lips twitching as they played catch-up with the sounds. "I've built you a vessel, back at my factory. I just need some time speaking with you, so the algorithm can learn your mannerisms, and—"

"Not going to happen," Guy told him.

The fixed face was unconcerned, not even looking straight at him.

"These," it said, one articulated hand making a smooth

gesture at Beaker and the assembled warriors. The hands, Amri noted, had been made with so much more understanding and care than any of the plastic faces she'd seen.

"They're what you left me with," Guy said sharply. "You and the others. When you decided to wreck me on the way down."

"You couldn't expect us to just sit back and let you get on with things," Gramm told him. "At least we were trying to recreate a living world in our chosen image. Not just a memorial."

"It was *not* just a memorial," Guy hissed, momentarily needled out of his composure. "It would have preserved us. Frozen. Waiting. And there was the beacon. Something would have come."

"Aliens." Even the artificial voice sounded derisive.

"Yes, why not? And they'd have come and found *us*. The greatest scions of Earth. They'd have found our stories, and understood what our minds could offer them. They'd have welcomed us. In a hundred years, a thousand, a million, *something* would have answered, and we'd have been ready."

"I will recreate the society we left," Gramm said placidly. "I would rather do so with you in it. Come on, Guy, what else have you got now?"

"I have what Matti put together, to screw you over, Pat," Guy said, leaning on the concrete table.

"He had nothing."

"He had it all. If I hadn't used Bruce's nasty little serum

to cut him off from his adoring populace, you'd be in grey goo territory already, and all your works. The plastic-eater, Pat. He cracked it. He was going to clean your pollution off the face of the world. How does the line go? 'Minute, invisible bacteria.'"

"You're bluffing," Gramm said, too quick, too emphatic.

"Not only am I not bluffing about the plastic-eater, I'm not bluffing about being able to access Matti's ant operating system, the very one I locked him out of. I've birthed a caste of ants that serve as perfect hosts for the bacterium, and they're ready to go." He turned around and signalled to Iffy. "Bring in exhibit A!"

The Cockroach and a couple of his pals hauled a sack over to the table and dumped out the contents. One of Gramm's Self-Driving People, or what was left of it. Something had eaten away at it like acid, leaving a weird lacework lattice behind, through which Amri could see innards similarly served. It reminded her of leaves where the insects had chewed away all the green but left the delicate veins intact.

Gramm's ambassador leapt up and stumbled back, more lifelike in that moment of panic than anything else in his whole kingdom. Guy laughed uproariously.

"It's been treated, hosed down, cleaned. It's quite safe. But as you can see, the test batch is quite voracious. If I let those ants go pop in your direction, well… it's *all* plastic thataways, isn't it?"

"You won't," Gramm said, his ambassador still keeping its distance from the table. "You *need* plastics. I know you. You won't want to live like an actual stone-age savage.

You'll build infrastructure, your damned beacon, all the rest of it. This will cripple you as much as me."

"No," Guy said. "It will cripple me *almost* as much as you. So sure, I'd *rather* be able to work towards a functioning technological culture, get all these guys trained up as technicians, get back to my big plans. But if it's a choice between barbarian warlord and plastic puppet, I know which I'll be plumping for. And so it comes down to this, Pat. Your current plan is to cover the Earth with that babbling shit you call a recreation of the old world. A plastic person in every pot.

"And we both know that's not compatible with anything else surviving. By the time you've finished, the air will be too polluted to breathe, too hot to endure, and you'll have rendered down all the biomass into plastics. Because it's not like there's much of a fossil fuel reserve left, but you can accelerate the process of turning living plants and animals and *people* into coal and oil.

"But I'm the god of that biomass now, Pat. I'm the god of the living. That biomass you want includes my worshippers. So your plan is off the table, and if need be, I'll melt the lot of you into stuff like this." A slap scattered the eaten-away pieces across the table.

"You're mad," Gramm's ambassador said. The jaw kept on mouthing the word over and over, silently.

"Ask Matti and Bruce how mad I am," Guy said. "Now you go and have a think and, when this marionette has something to say, it better include a surrender."

18.

WORDS OF POWER

OF COURSE THE ambassador didn't march back to its master with the news. It just stood there, and after a while everyone understood that Gramm was no longer actively inhabiting it. The god of plastics had gone off to think, and Guy, grinning, went to get a drink. There was already a mood of cautious celebration amongst the gathered warriors.

Amri sat on the edge of the concrete table, thinking that this place really was sacred now. This was where the good god had defeated the last of his evil brothers. This would be where tribes would come to settle differences, where someone like her could give out judgments in Guy's name. She liked the sound of that.

Beaker and Iffy came to join her, after a while. They'd heard most of it and she filled them in on the rest. They made an odd pair of maybe-allies. The stern old Seagull champion she'd been terrified of most of her days, with his unexpected inner life of scientific curiosity; the wild-haired, wide-eyed scarecrow of a Roach. Although, compared to their own addle-headed priest Failboy, Iffy was practically reasonable.

"Biomass." Beaker chewed over the term.

"Ain't the first time," Iffy put in. "All them gods go on about the biomass."

Beaker and Amri exchanged a look.

"He wants a temple," she said.

The Seagull's hard face was shorn of expression. "I mean, he's a god, isn't he? A temple seems a fitting thing for him to have."

After a little more talk, veiled and stepping carefully around any dangerous words, she went to find Guy. Beaker had lent her his mirror, which still held open the gateway to the wondrous library that Padreig Gramm tended.

"This is you," she told him.

"It's the man I was," he agreed. "When I was just a man."

The picture was that early one, him and those other people—not his fellow gods, but just people, smiling out at her. "Who are they?" she asked.

"Divine servants," Guy said grandly. "Angels. Valkyries. Fire giants." Searching her face for something, amusement or comprehension or gullibility. "All right, a lower tier of semi-divine beings is what I'm getting at. They were my team, my picked people. Those worthy of taking into space to build Utopia. The brightest minds Earth had to offer. People who could think beyond the miserly boundaries the world threw around them. Who could understand my vision. Good people. Smart people."

She licked dry lips, opened her mouth, paused, unsure

of how far she should go. Rabbit runs. Curiosity was for Seagulls. But she had to know.

"What happened to them?"

Guy looked past her at the table, at the skewed ambassador awaiting further instructions. "It's hard," he said at last, "living up to the expectations of a god. They weren't strong enough, in the end. One by one." The melancholy that touched him on occasion, that she had seen before. And she thought, *Utopia, the perfect world in space, how could they not thrive?* but at the same time she saw a lone suited figure trudging through a curving landscape that was shutting down section by section.

Biomass, she thought.

THE AMBASSADOR REANIMATED just as evening was coming on. Beaker had sent scouts with flags and lanterns off towards the territory Padreig Gramm had claimed, in case of any violent breach of diplomatic protocols, and the Cockroach had people down in the tunnels too. It seemed entirely possible that there was more plastic spine there than Guy had expected. And it wasn't as though that artificial body could actually look dejected, but Amri felt that there was something of that in it, as it returned to the table.

"You'll come round." Gramm's voice was flat. "When you've gotten bored playing to the cheap seats."

Guy shrugged. "Maybe."

"You'll get old," Gramm went on. "Even all those patent-pending organs of yours. In a hundred years. In two hundred.

I'll have solved the upload problem by then."

"The upload problem is that the upload isn't *us*," Guy said, sounding bored.

"It *can* be. I'll link brain and online running in parallel until you can segue seamlessly from meat to virtual. Until you forget all *this*…" A gesture at Guy, his body, the world. "Life as data, forever and forever, Guy. Who else can I share it with, but you?"

Guy shrugged. "Go share it with your Self-Driving People."

"Just… think about it. Grow old, play god, but remember. You'll see. You'll come round."

"But…?"

The automaton's hands twitched, fought with one another. One plastic finger pinged off and rattled across the table to be lost in the grass. For a moment Amri tensed, expecting an attack, but instead it was just some weird side-effect of the very human frustration on the far side of the link.

"But until then I will build a border," Gramm said. "A dome. About my lands. About my people. To protect them from you. To keep them safe. Until you're ready to join us. Let your vermin multiply and swarm. You'll grow tired of them."

"A theme park. Excellent. That's about your level," said Guy. "And in return I will stockpile a fuckton of plastic-eater ready to deploy when you try to backstab me. And don't think they won't eat their way through that dome."

"I won't," Gramm said. "I can wait, Guy. I'll perfect the upload and then I'll have all the time."

* * *

GRAMM DIDN'T BOTHER to reclaim the ambassador. Eventually Failboy would get spectacularly high and throw it in the river, letting it float off towards the distant sea for the King Crab people to marvel at.

"You trust him?" Beaker asked Guy. "The plastics god?"

"Not in the slightest. Next step is to infiltrate his network and keep tabs on just what he's doing, watch how the worm turns. But he'll be sulking for at least a week. That's how he is when he doesn't get his way. You'd better go tell your bully boys that they don't need to stick spears in anything."

Beaker nodded. "And what else do I tell them?" A glint of flint in his eye, squaring up to Guy a little. Amri held her breath.

"Tell them there's a god watching over them," Guy said simply. "A greater god, set over your birds and beasts and bugs. A god here on Earth who can protect them against Plastic Pat, and lead them into the future. A great future, Beaker. A future where we build that Made World you're so fond of. You want that, right? So, let's start here. Gather your people, gather all the people, send messengers to the rats and hedgehogs and raccoons and whatever the fuck else is out there. Tell them god's here, and you're with me or you're against me. With me, and you get to share in the future; against me and you get left to the past. Sound good to you? Because I want the Seagull as my right hand in this. Privileged position, Beaker."

For a moment Beaker just stood, face unreadable. Then his eyes squirrelled sideways, looking to Amri, looking to Iffy. Looking to the future, perhaps.

With a slight creaking of joints, he knelt. Bent his head. Prostrated himself before his god.

Guy beamed broadly, patted him on the head in benediction, spread his arms and beamed around at all the watching warriors, basking in their adulation.

"A temple," he said. "We need a temple, or how can we expect people to be impressed?"

Beaker straightened up, glanced at Amri again. "And your priestess?"

Guy nodded enthusiastically. "Yes. High priestess, a whole clergy. Screening my calls. Important god business only." He grinned again, and Amri smiled back, thinking of what Rabbit would say. *Find a place of safety, or else run.* But it was a long time since she had heard Rabbit speak to her, and Guy's voice was much louder.

"It shall be so," she said, and the others echoed her. She had never seen the future so clearly as in that moment.

19.

DEUS VULT

"The good god has spoken," Amri told the two Marsh Cat trackers. "There are poisons in the land you claim this year, perhaps next year. The year after you may fish there, but nobody must eat more than one fish from those pools in five days. The year after that, fish freely, and plant rice."

They eyed her, and each other, suspiciously. Marsh Cat was no real people, just a loose net drawn around a score of squabbling families. They'd trekked all the way to the city and the temple because they couldn't decide anything without it kicking off into a feud. They were new to the new gods, though. They didn't trust them, except maybe they trusted them more than they trusted each other.

Still, they'd offered tribute in advance, mostly dried fish, but copper, too—hanks of it torn from old junction boxes, proffered like transmuted straw. And the temple could always use copper, almost as much as it could gold. Because everything of the New-Made World needed metal, even if it used wood and other natural things instead of plastic. They could never know when the plastic might have to go away.

Having paid, the Marsh Cats were only cutting their own noses if they chose to go against the god's advice. They muttered and scowled, but at the same time they bowed and clasped their hands at her, and that would suffice.

And it was true; the god had spoken. She'd heard his words herself, the only one permitted into the deep sanctum of the temple. He hadn't been much concerned with the Marsh Cat's territorial ambitions, hadn't even heard of them, but he had spoken. The pronouncement was all, and it was up to her—after consulting with the wider priesthood about how far the divine changes had spread—to interpret what his words actually *meant*.

With the Cats backing out into the grand square, she took a moment to adjust her regalia. The armoured suit was tight about the bust, loose about the waist. Sitting on the throne of the high priestess, she looked properly regal. The costume bagged and sagged when she stood, though, a garment made for a large-framed man. Not for slight Amri, once the least toe of the Rabbit.

She had her assistants disrobe her and stow the armoured suit in its reliquary, ready for the next audience. In its place she dressed in wool, with a veil of transparent green plastic to afford her a little privacy. Her honour guard was waiting for her, parting the crowds of pilgrims as she crossed to the temple of the insect god.

The grand spire still stood there, and the paving of the ground was incised with radiating channels where the myriad messengers of that dead divinity coursed. More mounds were springing up all over the city and beyond, they said, and where they went, the feckless priesthood followed, claiming each as sacred and setting up their shrines that were part church and part suspect apothecary. All were linked to this hub, though.

It had been fifteen years since the tumultuous time when the new gods had first come to the earth. Fifteen good years and bad, but Guy's prophecy had come to pass, as the words of a god ought. The temple was the heart of the land, the focus of all the people Amri had ever heard of, and more beyond that. This holy city within the city was where the human world touched that of the divine. And who, in this hard world, could turn their back on the guidance of the gods?

Failboy met her at the steps to the stone and metal adjunct they'd built onto the ant spire. He was in one of his more serene moods, bowing before her, a mere grand priest before the high priestess herself. And gurning and grinning and taking none of it seriously, but that was Failboy for you, and sometimes she needed the reminder of just how much of it all was mummery.

She turned in the doorway to the insect god's shrine. About the grand square, the other temples loomed. The good god's great windowless stone mausoleum, the clear-sided box of the god of plastics and, for the long-dead plant god, a garden of exotic blooms, young trees and exciting fungi for Failboy to experiment with.

Inside, the others were already gathered. A modest meal

was laid out. Some bread, some fruit and dried meat, the new rice that grew so well, plus great bowls of curried insects, all set out on the concrete table that remained Most Sacred, so that only they, the senior priesthood, were permitted to eat off it. She was the last in, the business with the Marsh Cat having taken longer than she'd thought. Iffy was already crunching candied ants, half-lost in the wide robes of Failboy's chief acolyte and actual decision-maker. Hailfoot wore hardwearing clothes dyed green, his fingernails black with dirt from duties simultaneously ritual and practical. For the plastic god, Beaker wore his corslet of mirrors, a tessellation of flat, hand-sized lozenges that let him transmit the god's forward-looking message—which was Beaker's message—to the faithful through light and sound. All dull grey now, because everyone here was already initiated into the mystery.

And nobody had exactly sat down to work out how to tell the tale. It told itself, and somehow didn't double back or contradict itself or leave threads the less faithful might tug on to unravel it. The story had gone out across the city, and then beyond the city, and then beyond that, so that even the King Crab of the coast and the far northern Blood Squirrel people sent nervous emissaries with gifts for the divine.

Four gods had come to the world to remake it. To return life to it and create a paradise where once there had been a wasteland. And that was true. Four gods had granted their gifts to the people of the land, and there the truth strained a little, because Amri and the other senior priests knew damn well they hadn't intended to. Years ago now, a decade and a half, but she remembered the blind hunger of the plant god tearing up the land, the monstrous dissections of Fabrey's ants. The coming of the gods had set all the people of the world in the shadow of extinction, none of them visible in any of those divine futures.

And yet the ever-growing roots of the plants which Bruce Mayall had planted purified the water so it could be drunk. The swarming ants of Matthias Fabrey were protein and sustenance to the hungry. Within the spire, other specialist castes of insect provided ongoing and hereditary access to the ability to produce chemicals and materials not found in nature, and thanks to the good god's intervention, Iffy and the Cockroach could give them commands and harvest their secretions. A sacred duty Amri was more than happy to leave to them.

And as for Padreig Gramm, he continued on, the only other god still to walk the earth. His grand dome kingdom had shrunk and shrunk after repeated incursions and threats to deploy the plastic-eater, until he paced that little lit-up box across the square, deprived of his plastic people, left only with the running of the great server farm that gave them access to the knowledge and marvels of the Made World. The world that they were, by their own slow efforts, remaking. Gramm still claimed to be on the cusp of solving the upload problem, but those claims hadn't changed markedly in ten years. He still thought that his ongoing imprisonment and exhibition was at Guy's express command. Amri felt it was kinder that way. It made the plastic god feel important.

And there was Guy Vesten himself, of course.

He had been happy with the temple, its grand, foreboding frontage. Its statement that *Here Is Power*. The unceasing work all the peoples had put into that monument to his grandeur. He had even approved the maze beneath.

Parting him from the magic suit had not been hard. Had not even been novel. From early in their acquaintance, Amri's physical companionship had been just one more due he had accepted, part of being a god. He'd fought, when Beaker and the others had seized him. Fought, and shown remarkable strength in his desperation. But what Beaker lacked in artificial enhancement, he made up for in a lifetime of fighting dirty.

She knew her role as high priestess was mummery, of course, but at the same time she believed it. When delegations came seeking the wisdom of the good god, she always retreated down to the lowest, most sacred sanctum of the temple and listened for him. His voice would rise up to her, begging, imploring, desperate. He would promise her anything but, as with any supernatural thing caged, she knew better than to believe any of it. Sometimes the genie is imprisoned for good reason.

"I know what your dream was," she called down to him once. "It had no more room for us than the plant god's or the others'. A monument to yourself, a beacon to the stars. A frozen world to preserve your greatness."

"I didn't know!" he howled back. "I didn't know you were there!"

But she remembered *Biomass*, the word the gods had used for the raw materials they would build their paradises out of, now that the paradise they had built in the sky had fallen to ruin and the graves of all who had followed them up there. *Biomass*, and doubtless he'd say it was just animals, plants, the scum off the rivers and the slime of the beaches, but she knew it meant her and everyone she knew and everyone like them. Because they'd had the bad grace to survive the gods' departure, and such apostasy couldn't be tolerated.

"You knew," she whispered down to the god. "You always knew about us. But until the others cast you down here, you didn't care." And she'd walked away, but she'd made sure that food and water were lowered down to him every day. He was the god, after all. He was entitled to such offerings.

Beaker was talking about new irrigation channels, to bring the sweet water further out from the city. To fight plague and raise crops. Hailfoot sketched out a map on the sacred table, using a finger dipped in the new batch of beer, showing how the will of the plant god could be best extended into the next tribe's lands, and the next. Considering what they should ask as recompense, whether the Marsh Cat or the Blight Pigeon or the Bleach Crow should be made to build a local temple, so the priesthood could keep a lid on their arguing. Amri leant back and picked at the food, feeling herself amongst family as she never had with the Rabbit, not since she was very small indeed.

Acknowledgements

WITH THANKS TO Simon and Oliver at the agency, and to everyone at Solaris.

FIND US ONLINE!

www.rebellionpublishing.com

/solarisbooks

/solarisbks

/solarisbooks

/solarisbooks.bsky.social

SIGN UP TO OUR NEWSLETTER!

rebellionpublishing.com/newsletter

YOUR REVIEWS MATTER!

Enjoy this book? Got something to say?

Leave a review on Amazon, GoodReads or with your favourite bookseller and let the world know!